'I'll have y[...]
door befo[...]

Gemma tensed. 'Sure you will,' she conceded. 'I'll be hammering with a feather and I won't have to do it twice, will I? Because you'll be waiting eagerly enough, and you won't have torment on your mind.'

Felipe's face darkened. 'Sleep well, *querida*,' he said, controlled and immobile. 'And prepare yourself for the onslaught. It's not a threat but a promise.'

Dear Reader

Autumn's here and the nights are drawing in—but when better to settle down with your favourite romances? This month, Mills & Boon have made sure that you won't notice the colder weather—our wide range of love stories are sure to warm the chilliest of hearts! Whether you're wanting a rattling good read, something sweet and magical, or to be carried off to hot, sunny countries—like Australia, Greece or Venezuela—we've got the books to please you.

Enjoy!

The Editor

Natalie Fox was born and brought up in London and has a daughter, two sons and two grandsons. Her husband, Ian, is a retired advertising executive, and they now live in a tiny Welsh village. Natalie is passionate about her three cats, two of them strays brought back from Spain where she lived for five years, and equally passionate about gardening and writing romance. Natalie says she took up writing because she absolutely *hates* going out to work!

Recent titles by the same author:

RELUCTANT MISTRESS
OFFER ME A RAINBOW
REVENGE

LOVE IN TORMENT

BY

NATALIE FOX

MILLS & BOON LIMITED
ETON HOUSE 18-24 PARADISE ROAD
RICHMOND SURREY TW9 1SR

*First published in Great Britain 1992
by Mills & Boon Limited*

© Natalie Fox 1992

*Australian copyright 1992
Philippine copyright 1992
This edition 1992*

ISBN 0 263 77795 2

*Set in Times Roman 10½ on 12 pt.
01-9211-52137 C*

Made and printed in Great Britain

CHAPTER ONE

'You can't go! It's out of the question!' Isobel Soames had cried. 'Gemma, I absolutely forbid it!'

Gemma would never forget those words as long as she lived. The forerunners of what was to come to crumble her world. Another shock, the second of recent months that would stamp her twenty-sixth year as the most emotionally traumatic of her life.

Even now, staring blindly out of the window of the Tropicana hotel in the heart of heat-hazed Caracas, she couldn't decide which shock had hit hardest: losing Felipe, the only man she had ever loved, or finding that the man she had called 'Daddy' all her life hadn't been her father at all!

'Mother,' Gemma had argued formally, 'the travel arrangements have been made. I have accepted this commission and I'm going to do it...'

'There will be other commissions. You're talented and in a position to pick your own clients. I don't want you to go to Venezuela!'

It was on the occasion of one of Gemma's fort-nightly visits to her mother at the family home in Surrey, usually so amiable and packed with art-world gossip, but not this time. Gemma's news that she had been commissioned to paint the portrait of one of Venezuela's oil barons had not filled her mother with delight as she had anticipated. Far from it; her mother's face had frozen in shock and then had come the fury.

Shocked herself, Gemma had gaped at her mother as she'd paced the drawing-room of Whitegates. Her mother had never stood in her way before. On the contrary, she'd been delighted when Gemma had echoed her own artistic talent. Their professions lay in different directions, though. Isobel was society's favourite interior designer and had been for the last two decades, whereas Gemma's career had veered towards portraiture. People interested her more than the trappings they surrounded themselves with. It had never caused dissent between them before.

'South America isn't another planet——' Gemma had protested.

'South America isn't the problem!' Isobel had snapped, clutching her shoulders, her painted nails digging into the fine silk of her blouse. Then her whole body had sagged and when she had turned to Gemma she seemed to have aged desperately. She was still beautiful, of course, classically elegant with sculptured features that were timeless. Her dark hair, tinted now to banish the wisps of grey at her temples, was drawn back into a tight coil of twisted silk. The eyes suddenly aged her, Gemma had thought at that moment. Normally so clear and bright, as deep a brown as Gemma's own, they were now misted painfully.

'It's not the place, Gemma, darling, it's the man,' she had husked painfully.

'The man? Agustín Delgado de Navas, one of the richest oil men in South America? How can you possibly object to *him*?' Gemma had cried in amazement.

She remembered the silence that had preceded her mother's reply more than anything else. That awful, aching gap where considerations were weighed and a decision made to tell or not.

'He's your father,' had come the flat statement that had so brutally stunned Gemma. Those few crippling words that had torn at her heart, which had already suffered so badly in the past months.

'He's your father' . . . the words echoed and echoed in Gemma's head. Were still echoing now, halfway round the world and weeks later.

Gemma crossed the hotel room and impatiently snapped off the air-conditioning. She poured herself a cold drink from the courtesy bar, slid open the patio doors of the balcony and was immediately swamped by a heat that took her breath away. She gasped, quickly acclimatised then slumped down in a cane chair and closed her eyes wearily, unaware of the city traffic thundering ten floors below in the tropical metropolis.

She had defied her mother and now here she was, waiting in Caracas for her escort for the last stage of her journey, a short flight in comparison to the long haul from Heathrow. Private jet from Caracas, over the mountains to the plains of Loma de Grande and the Villa Verde where she would come face to face with the man who was her father but would never know it.

'If you insist on going, Gemma, you must promise me you'll not reveal your true identity,' Isobel had bargained.

'Just what is my true identity? A Soames, a Villiers, a de Navas?' Gemma had questioned bitterly. 'For nearly twenty-six years I've believed myself a Soames; now I find I'm the offspring of some dubious Latin oil baron——'

'You are a Soames,' Isobel had interjected levelly. 'And don't you ever forget it. Peter adopted you and thought of you as his own. He loved you and cherished you.'

'But he wasn't my *real* father,' Gemma had croaked, her eyes bright with unshed tears. 'How could you have cheated me so?' She had bitten her lip miserably and looked at her mother. If she thought she was suffering, she could imagine what her mother was going through. 'I'm sorry,' she'd whispered, regretting hurting her mother with her outburst. 'It's such a shock . . . I can hardly believe it. But I want to know everything. Tell me, Mother, everything.'

Gemma had listened without interruption. The irony of it all had amazed her. The story her mother related was almost a carbon copy of her own affair with Felipe, with one exception. Agustín had left his lover not knowing she was carrying his child. Felipe had left Gemma with nothing—though a broken heart could hardly be described as nothing.

Was it a cliché associated with all South American men—love 'em and leave 'em? And how strange that she had fallen for the same type of charismatic man her mother had.

Isobel Soames had spared nothing; it was a story so poignantly paralleled with her own affair with Felipe that soon Gemma was in tears.

'Would you have told me all this if Daddy was still alive?' she had murmured at last. At seventeen she had mourned his death not knowing he wasn't her own. Even knowing the truth now didn't alter the love she held for him. He'd been a wonderful father.

'No, I wouldn't,' Isobel had answered honestly. 'Your father loved you and you loved him. I saw no

reason to make waves in our life. There were no more
children to come after you... it was a difficult birth
and...and, well, Peter loved me enough not to mind.'

'And did you love him?'

'Yes,' her mother had insisted quickly, and then
sighed. 'Of course I loved him, we'd been friends for
a long time, but not like——'

'Not like my real father?' Gemma had finished for
her, furiously swinging her long black hair away from
her face. Her moods had been lurching dangerously
from anger to sadness as her mother talked. Some of
the time she'd understood, sometimes she just hadn't.

'My love for Agustín was quite different, Gemma,'
Isobel had said softly. 'A once-in-a-lifetime love, never
to be repeated at such a depth. The day he went back
to South America was the worst of my life. He said
he would send for me, but he didn't.'

'And yet you let him go, you just let him walk out
of your life!' Gemma had protested hotly. 'You were
pregnant with me and you didn't even put up a fight
for him? He didn't even know you were carrying his
child?'

Even as the words had spurted angrily from her
mouth she'd known why her mother hadn't fought
for the man she loved. Hadn't she done the very same
thing herself? Let Felipe go because pride and confusion and the sting of betrayal had bitten so deeply
into her soul, scarring her so deeply that grovelling
was out of the question.

Pride. She was as deeply imbued with it as her
mother. Felipe had been there one day, gone the next,
Bianca, his stunning cousin, along with him. A week
later he'd left a message on her answerphone, to
contact him on a New York phone number. She

hadn't, of course. He'd walked out and left her, taken
Bianca with him, hadn't he? All she had was a re-
corded message, cryptic and to the point, no words
of love or missing her, no inflexion of caring in the
tone of his voice. God knew, she'd played it back
enough times, each time hoping to find what she was
seeking, some small hint of their past love, their week
of love and passion. She had found nothing.

'How long did your affair last?' she had asked her
mother.

'Six months. The most wonderful months of my
life.'

That was the subtle difference, Gemma dismally
thought as she went back into her hotel room now to
shower away the stickiness of the tropical heat. Her
affair with Felipe was a drop in the ocean compared
to her mother's and Agustín's. Six months was long
enough to form a deep, lasting relationship, for all
the good it had done her mother, but a solitary week
barely touched the perimeters of real love; so the
agony aunts would have you believe.

Gemma knew better. She had given Felipe her heart
and soul. She'd not led a sheltered life; her mother's
career alone had seen to that. There had been social
gatherings at Whitegates that had broadened her
mind, packed full as they were with the so-called
beautiful people. Her father's friends too, academics
from the university, writers, poets, philosophers. And
her own career had hardly been without event. Her
first one-woman exhibition in the much acclaimed
Portia Gallery in Paris had set the ball rolling. Nepotism, one cruel art critic had pronounced in a Sunday
paper known for its hardline tactics with new artists,
but nepotism had nothing to do with the commissions

that poured in. Gemma was mature and wise enough to know she had talent. A pity that wisdom and maturity didn't follow through in her personal life. Yes, she'd seen life, but it hadn't helped her where Felipe was concerned.

Gemma towel-dried her hair and combed it through in front of the dressing-table mirror. It had grown long since that week with Felipe in London, and now hung like a sable curtain beyond her shoulders. Straight like her mother's, thick and glossy too, but there the likeness ended. Her mother's beauty was classical whereas Gemma's was softer. Her lips fuller, not nearly so well defined, and her large brown eyes more limpid and fawn-like than Isobel's. Vulnerability—did that have something to do with the difference in their looks? Whatever, they weren't alike and in the circumstances it was a blessing. Agustín would never associate her with his mistress of the past.

Gemma peered at herself more closely. She *was* vulnerable, but hadn't been before Felipe. Once she had handled her associations with men with detached aplomb. Felipe had changed all that with a single glance across a crowded gallery floor on the opening night of her London exhibition. Their eyes had met and Gemma, who had never believed in such a thing as love at first sight, had fallen as if she had been flung from Westminster Bridge with lead weights round her ankles.

'I like your work,' he'd said after battling his way through the crowds to reach her. His dark, nocturnal eyes held hers and everyone and everything around them faded away into nonentity.

'Thank you,' she'd murmured, and he'd smiled.

'Can I do us both a favour and whisk us away from all this? I want to make love to you,' he'd husked softly.

She hadn't even been surprised at his outspokenness, it had just seemed so right. He'd taken over her life in a brief, blatantly honest exchange of words and taken her elbow and guided her out into the cold, wintry London night.

There was no pre-nuptial dinner to melt her reserves, no voyage into pasts to get to know each other better, nothing but the feeling that it was right and beautiful and so very exciting. He held her hand in the back of the taxi, this tall, dark, enigmatic stranger. Her experienced artist's eye registered beauty beyond compare, deep-set sultry eyes that hinted of Hispanic descent, an aquiline nose so perfectly proportioned above a mouth that was strong yet sensuous. His hair was as black as a moonless night and she knew that when she touched it the tight curls under the tips of her fingers would spring like coils of eastern silk.

Felipe Santos was the most perfect of lovers. Only one small doubt wavered hesitantly within Gemma when they reached his mews house in St John's Wood. Never in her life had she done this, given herself to a man without thought to the consequences. But it was a passing hesitation, as swift as a cloud powered away by the wind of change.

He took her in his arms as soon as he had shut the door behind them. His mouth was warm and tender, no hint yet of the power of his passion, the near violence of his lovemaking.

'You're the most beautiful animal I have ever seen,' he grated at her throat, and Gemma smiled. No man had ever compared her to an animal before, and her excitement mounted.

He led her up to his sumptuous bedroom, which was thickly carpeted and furnished with swags of silk hung at the windows. There were warm antiques and the bed was huge, soft and inviting, draped in heavily embroidered blue silk. A lover's bedroom.

Felipe undressed her, stripping the black silk lace from her trembling body, the act almost a ritual with softly spoken words of adoration for her creamy skin, and the perfection of her firm round breasts.

'I will make love to you every day of my life,' he murmured throatily. 'Whether we are together or apart, in the flesh or in my mind, but every day I will possess you.'

No man could compare to this one. He was unique, charismatic, hedonistic in his approach to sexuality.

She watched in awe as he removed his own clothes, peeling off his evening suit and shirt to reveal a body as perfect and faultless as any Rodin sculpture. Smooth bronzed skin, dark curly hair that massed his chest, narrowing down his stomach in a column of hazy blackness to his groin. The need to touch was overpowering but part of his ritual was to wait, to suspend the feeling-need till the moment was right.

Eventually he stretched his hands out to her and she took them and slowly he drew her into his arms, drawing her into his power, into the heady realms of a world she had never known before.

He carried her to the sensual bed, and laid her down. His tongue explored, lightly at first, and then his urgency powered them both to a fierce eroticism that swam them into a haze of white-hot passion.

Her breasts ached with her need, her heart pounded fiercely with the depth of that need. Her body wasn't her own. It floated mystically under his touch then rose in flames of desire as he entered her for the first time, driving hard into her, groaning her name over and over till it became a primeval incantation deep in his throat.

Their need for each other was insatiable that first night. They made love till dawn then made love again. They slept and murmured words of love to each other, lay in each other's arms wondering at all that was happening to them. Later, they rose, showered, drank sweet thick Turkish coffee, talked quietly, made love on the soft leather sofa downstairs in the lounge.

The hours ran into days and Gemma forgot work and all that passed for her life before Felipe. They were both cocooned in their ethereal, perfumed love-nest, oblivious to outside intervention. Then Bianca arrived. Rich, angry and beautiful Bianca.

'You were supposed to pick me up from the airport, Felipe!' she cried when Felipe answered the door to her one morning. 'Pay the taxi, will you?' she ordered, thrusting her way into the house.

Gemma stood at the top of the elegant spiral staircase watching this scene below, too afraid to move, her heart racing. It didn't stop racing when Felipe urged her down to meet his cousin who had just flown in from New York.

Cousin—it didn't help somehow. Bianca was exotically beautiful, so was Felipe, and, cousins or not, the look Bianca gave Felipe was one of raw anger, and it had little to do with arriving at Heathrow and having to hail a taxi to St John's Wood.

Felipe was unaware of his cousin's hostility to Gemma; men often didn't see what was obvious to another woman. But Gemma registered every look, every adverse vibration the girl gave off. She was younger than Gemma but exuded that mature air common to women who were beautiful, rich and spoilt.

'So this is your excuse for not meeting me, is it?' She flicked her eyes frostily over Gemma and slid out of her feather-weight cashmere coat, letting it fall carelessly over the sofa. 'I might have known. No thought of me sweating it out at the airport, hanging around waiting——'

'I forgot,' Felipe interjected with a tolerant smile.

'Well, damn you! I need sleep. I'm exhausted. Don't wake me.' With that she swept upstairs, slamming the door of the guest bedroom behind her.

'I'd better go,' Gemma murmured uncomfortably.

'Like hell you will!' Felipe grated, pulling her into his arms.

'Don't, Felipe, not with——'

'Not with Bianca in the house? Why so suddenly prudish?'

'I'm not!'

'Forget her, then . . .'

'As you forgot to pick her up from the airport?'

'Is it any wonder?' He grinned down at her. 'Since you, I've forgotten there was a life before.'

His kiss melted away her doubts and she stayed, for a while.

Suddenly they were a threesome. Felipe took them both out to dinner that night and was charming and sweet, secretly squeezing Gemma's hand yet dividing his conversation equally between the two women.

Gemma didn't return to the mews house with them but diplomatically insisted on getting a taxi to her home and studio in Maida Vale.

'I'll call you first thing in the morning,' Felipe told her outside the restaurant, not arguing with her but kissing her tenderly. Somehow that kiss had seemed so final.

But the next morning, true to his word, he phoned and sent flowers. Later he came round to the studio, saying how much he had missed her, and she locked all thoughts of Bianca away in the depths of her mind.

She showed him the latest project she was working on, a portrait of an industrialist for some élite boardroom.

'He looks boring and pompous,' Felipe told her, without meaning to offend.

'He is,' Gemma told him abruptly, and he swept her into his arms to kiss away her petulance.

'You're offended?' he laughed.

'Not at all. I paint what I see.'

'Paint me.'

'Never!' She grinned. 'I don't do animal portraits!'

He growled at her neck then and they laughed and everything was suddenly all right. Later she cooked supper and he stayed all night, loving her till the small hours as if Bianca had never been part of the last two days. Gemma didn't mention her; it would have been an intrusion on something so very special between them. There was only herself and Felipe and their love in the whole wide world ...

She'd never seen him again after that. He'd left her at lunchtime, promising to call her later, but he hadn't. The next day she had driven to the mews house in St John's Wood, Felipe's London home when he was in the country. She'd sat in the car and stared up at the house, just knowing it was empty. He'd gone and so had Bianca.

A week later had come the call from New York, but by then it was too late. Gemma had suffered enough.

Gemma glanced at her watch now and frowned. Her escort was late and she was restless and bored but there was little choice but to sit tight and wait. It was too hot to wander the streets of Caracas, and if she did venture out into the soporific heat she might miss Mike Anders, her father's pilot, who was to fly her the last leg of her journey.

Gemma shivered. She mustn't think of him as her father; he was a client, a Venezuelan oil man, nothing more, nothing less.

The phone purred and Gemma lifted it. 'Thank you, I'll be right down.'

She swung her leather satchel with her brushes and oils over her shoulder and wheeled her suitcase to the lifts. She'd faxed through her other requirements to the Villa Verde: an easel and several canvases. She didn't know yet what sort of conditions she was expected to work under. A proper studio with the correct light was ideal but on these sort of assignments, in the client's own home, she would have to make do.

'Sorry to have kept you waiting, Miss Soames...'

'Call me Gemma.' She smiled at the young American pilot, who was cool, blond and sporty.

'Gemma it is,' he grinned back. 'Pretty heavy schedule today, I'm afraid—that's why I'm late. Flew de Navas out to Maracaibo last night and just got back this morning. One helluva problem out there—

massive oil leak as they were loading one of the tankers. No doubt the ole man will sort it all out.'

'He's still there?' Gemma frowned. She wanted to start as soon as possible, as she had other commissions waiting back in the UK.

'Yeah, he won't leave till it's under control. Hey, don't worry, be happy, plenty to keep you buzzing out at the ranch,' he laughed, ushering her into a taxi to the airport. 'Pool, horses, tennis, shooting; you name it, they got it. Hey, are you really going to paint the old man? Queer sort of a job for a woman, ain't it?'

Gemma was glad of his company. Hadn't Wordsworth waxed lyrical about the bliss of solitude? He'd obviously never been holed up in blistering Caracas trying not to think of people he'd rather forget. 'They' troubled her mind at this very moment in spite of Mike's boisterous running commentary as they hurtled through the busy streets of Caracas. Agustín would probably have a wife and a family. It was one of the arguments her mother had put up to try to stop her coming.

'You'll only hurt yourself when you meet his family. You can't do it, Gemma. Leave things as they are.'

Gemma had shaken her head determinedly. 'I can't be hurt, Mother, not any more. I don't know him, he's a stranger to me but I have to go, more so now after what you've told me. He's my father; I'm curious. Can't you understand that?'

She had at last, but hadn't given Gemma her blessing; that was too painful for her.

She still loves him, Gemma thought as Mike loaded her suitcase and satchel into the Lear jet, after twenty-

six years and life with another man she still loves him.
Somehow she understood.

The mountains beyond Caracas were enthralling,
threatening and savage. Mike kept up his commentary, unknowingly diverting Gemma away from
her own troubled thoughts. She talked herself into
thinking it was a good thing Agustín wouldn't be there
to meet her. She wasn't ready yet, but would she ever
be?

'There she blows!' Mike laughed, tapping the
window to the left as they lost height and powered
down over green plains, far lusher than Gemma had
expected.

'Quite a spread, isn't it?'

Gemma nodded, mute with awe. Southfork paled
into insignificance. This was how *real* oil barons lived.
The Villa Verde was the centre piece of the massive
hacienda. And was that a church, the white-washed
building closest to the impressive villa? Bright blue
caught her eye as they swung down low over the estate,
bright blue of a pool shaded by palms and dark green
cypresses.

There were cottages dotted around and Gemma
wondered if they all belonged to the man whose
portrait she had come to paint. It was more like a
village than one man's home. So maybe he had a large
family, sons and daughters with their own families.
Suddenly she didn't want to be here, wished she had
heeded her mother's advice.

Registering her sudden look of concern Mike misinterpreted it. 'Don't worry,' he laughed, unbuckling
his seatbelt after they had landed smoothly on the
airstrip far away from the hacienda, 'you're not expected to walk to the villa.'

'I'm glad of that,' Gemma smiled as Mike slid open the door and a furnace of heat assailed her. 'It's hotter than Caracas.'

'Hell isn't hotter than Caracas,' Mike joked.

They walked to the hangar and Mike hauled her case into the back seat of an open-topped Chevrolet. 'Hop in, and we'll be there in no time.'

They were. Mike drew to a halt in front of the palatial stone steps at the front of the Villa Verde and Gemma slid out of her seat and stared up at the sprawling two-storey house. It was gleaming white, rough-plastered in some age-old traditional way, its roof capped with antique tiles of shiny green. The shutters at the windows were ornate and painted green to match the roof. The old villa looked cool and just a little imposing—or was it her ragged nerves that gave the impression of the world closing in around her?

A short, dark, middle-aged woman, clothed in the customary black of a widow, came out of the huge studded double doors of the house and stood waiting for Gemma.

'Señorita Soames, I am happy to greet you. I am Maria.' She smiled and put a hand out to Gemma, which she took. 'You are tired, *si*? I show you your room and then you eat and rest.' She turned to Mike as he strode into the huge reception hall with Gemma's suitcase, his trainers squeaking on the highly polished terracotta floor tiles. 'Christina, she wait in the kitchen for you. She miss you.' Maria grinned and winked at Gemma.

Mike dropped Gemma's suitcase at the foot of the great stone stairway with its wrought-iron banister of twisted vines coiling up to the upper floor. He turned and grinned at the two women. 'Misses me, eh? And so she should.' With that he disappeared down a long corridor, a definite spring in his step.

Maria laughed. 'Love, eh? Is good, *si*? Christina is my daughter. She love the Americano. Come, I take you up. Pepe will bring the case.'

Gemma, clutching her precious satchel, followed Maria upstairs, gazing in awe at the huge paintings that hung from the rough-plastered walls. A lot of them were portraits, which Gemma promised herself she'd study more closely later. For the moment all she wanted to do was get unpacked and cool off, though the house was cool enough; pretty dark too, she noted. The windows were all narrow and some of them shuttered to keep out the heat of the sun. She wondered where she would be expected to work and hoped that wherever it was there was more light than was being allowed to filter in the vaulted hallway and the stairs.

It was a huge villa, much bigger inside than it appeared outside. It was almost medieval in its décor, the stark white walls hung with what looked like iron objects of torture but were probably antique farming implements. All it needed was a couple of strategically placed suits of armour and she would feel she was in a castle of the Middle Ages. Heavens! There they were, round the next corner. Gemma skirted them warily, suppressing a grin.

Her room was coolly furnished, the bed an ornate affair with carved nymphs twirling vines around their heads on the mahogany headboard. It was draped with a creamy lace bedspread and there were matching lace drapes at the two narrow windows. There were huge rugs on the stone floor, pale orange with Aztec designs in blues and cream. The furniture, deeply carved wardrobes and chests of drawers, were heavy and

ponderous but not unpleasant to live with. The room
was scented with roses, which was nice, though the
vases were filled with exotic waxy orchids in vibrant
blues which gave off no smell. A Caribbean fan
throbbed dully above the bed.

'It's lovely,' Gemma breathed, slipping her satchel
from her shoulder. It wasn't her taste in décor but she
nevertheless acknowledged it to be a beautiful room.
Her mother would have adored it.

'The bathroom, too.' Maria smiled proudly, opening
a heavy wooden door across the room.

Gemma peered in to see a wealth of marble and
gold dolphin taps and sparkling mirrors.

'It's perfect,' she smiled, as a small, leathered Pepe
delivered her suitcase to the room she would occupy
till the portrait was finished.

'I unpack for you,' Maria said, stepping to the case
as Pepe went out of the room.

'No, Maria. Thank you, but I can manage.' Gemma
wanted to be alone, to get her emotions together. She
was here, in her father's house, and it all felt very
strange.

'I leave you, then. I bring food to the terrace when
you are ready.'

Gemma stood by the window when she was alone
and gazed down over the gardens at the back of the
villa. Lush tropical gardens full of colour and
brightness. Flagstoned paths trailed through beds of
roses; no doubt where the perfume came from,
Gemma mused, breathing deeply. The swimming-pool
lay beyond a screen of cypresses. Gemma could see
the gleam of blue through the dark green and longed
to cool her travel-weary body. She turned to her
suitcase—first things first . . .

She stood frozen in time, half turned away from the window. A figure stood in the doorway of the bedroom. A figure she knew so well, but the apparition was some cruel trick of the dim light, surely, accentuated by this sombre old villa. It moved, came towards her, and Gemma's hand shot to her mouth to stem the half-scream that rose in her throat.

'It's not possible!' she breathed at last as the apparition stopped in front of her.

'Anything is possible in my world,' Felipe breathed heavily, 'especially if you are fired by revenge and have the resources to avenge a betrayal.'

Stunned, Gemma stared up at him, too devastated to think straight. How, why...?

'You look shocked, my darling. Have I changed so very much since last we loved?'

Her heart strained at her ribcage till she thought it would burst through the fragility of her bones. Oh, God, he had changed. He was thinner and gaunter than before. There was no love in his eyes, no love in his harsh voice though he talked of love.

'I don't understand,' she grated at last, her eyes warily searching his for some answer. There was such menace in the dark depths of them that she shook her head to try and dispel the terror of it. Why? Why was he here?

'I don't suppose for a minute you do,' he said slowly, bringing his hand up to tilt her chin. He laughed softly at the fear in her eyes. 'I've brought you here for one purpose, sweet one: to torment you the way you tormented me. No woman does that to me, no woman twists my emotions till they are left wrung dry like a discarded rag...'

'Felipe,' Gemma cried, her eyes misted and wide. She couldn't think, didn't understand what was happening. He was the last person she expected to see here at her father's home.

'Did ... did you arrange all this?' was her first coherent question. He had to have done; coincidence didn't stretch to these limits. The commission had been arranged through her agent, direct from the wealthy Venezuelan himself, so she had supposed.

'Naturally. It was the only way I could get you here. You wouldn't have come otherwise, would you? Or maybe you would. You came to me easily enough once before,' he breathed cruelly.

The pain of those words cut deep into Gemma. What was powering this cruelty?

Running her tongue over her dry lips, she forced words to her mouth. 'I still don't understand. You talk of revenge, betrayal. What did I do to deserve such treatment?'

Somehow it seemed doubly painful to Gemma. She had thought she had been asked here to paint a portrait of the man she now knew to be her father. It was obvious now she wasn't. It had been a trick, a ruse to get her here ... but ... but Mike had known her purpose, and surely he wasn't in on this cruel deception?

'You obviously do not know our ways. Women here do not treat South American men the way you treated me. Women know their place, and you will know your place in time, *querida*.' His hand snaked up behind her neck and pulled her towards him in a swift movement that gave Gemma no chance to protest.

His mouth crushed hers and it was as if a stranger was the perpetrator. This wasn't the man she had loved so desperately. There was no tenderness, no passion, merely harsh pain that grazed her lips brutally. She tore herself away from him, her lips burning, her mind buzzing dully. She had loved this man once, truly loved him, and now he struck fear and confusion inside her.

'Don't you ever touch me like that again,' she cried, desperately controlling the tremor in her voice. 'I don't know what's happened to you——'

His eyes narrowed warningly. 'Well, you will, Gemma. I will show you, in words and deeds. I will drive you to the limits of your desire and then I will discard you as you discarded me. Torment—you will know the true meaning of the word by the time I have finished with you.' He smiled cynically. 'You will learn, and it won't be a pleasant lesson, I assure you.' With that he turned on his heel and strode from the room, leaving Gemma mortally afraid for her sanity and her life.

CHAPTER TWO

GEMMA couldn't move with shock, though her mind suddenly put a spurt on as if it had a sudden tail-wind behind it. She had never seen this side of Felipe before and she didn't like it. He terrified her. He had loved her once but Bianca had come between them, so why was he suddenly making such wicked threats to hurt her?

Slowly the life came back to her numbed body and she moved, hesitantly, though. He had shaken her and the shock waves thrummed through her nerves, stretching them crazily till her whole body seemed to ache with fear. She crossed to her suitcase and stared at it blankly, her eyes wide. For once in her life she was terribly unsure of herself, even unsure what to do. Should she unpack? There was no commission, no portrait to be painted. She was here on a fool's errand, manipulated by her former lover who seemed hell-bent on some sort of revenge.

Clenching her fists tightly, she braced herself. She had to find out what was going on and there was no time like the present. She didn't bother to change but flew out of the room in the clothes she had travelled from Caracas in, thin white cotton jeans, crumpled in the heat of the day, and a loose, wispy black top that flapped around her midriff as she ran.

She didn't know where to find him but find him she must. Damn this place, it was like a maze. She ran down the stone stairs and out into bright sunlight, blinking her eyes against the fierce sun.

Not a human soul to be seen. Gemma bit her lip and walked to the end of the villa, calmer now but still uncertain. Maria had said something about a terrace which must be at the back of the house.

She rounded the villa and saw wrought-iron tables and chairs, shady umbrellas—and Felipe.

Determinedly she walked towards him, mouthing questions in her mind, trying to find answers before she spoke them.

He was standing looking over a low stone wall that enclosed the terrace, hands plunged deep into the pockets of white linen trousers. There was a slight breeze which ruffled his short-sleeved shirt, otherwise he might have been as stiff as one of the stone statues that decorated the patio.

'Felipe, we must talk,' she murmured behind him.

'Must we?' he drawled, not turning to face her. 'From what I remember we didn't do much of that before. We spent our time in bed, locked in each other's arms.'

There was a step behind them and Gemma whirled, startled by the sudden intrusion into the bitter-sweet memories Felipe had evoked. Locked in each other's arms. She had wanted to die there, wrapped around his body, his around hers. Drifting in and out of sleep and passion. Days and days of love and laughter and more love. Had she dreamed it all? Now, standing here on this tropical terrace, a million miles away from home, her lover's implacable shoulders turned away from her, she imagined she had. She shivered with trepidation and watched Maria place a silver tray of food and drink down on one of the tables.

'Felipe, you eat with Señorita Soames?'

'No, thank you, Maria. I'll eat later. Bring me a brandy, though.'

Gemma's mouth dropped open at the familiar exchange between the two. She waited till Maria laid out cutlery, salad and cold meats for her and when she stepped back into the villa Gemma spoke.

'She called you Felipe . . .'

'Why shouldn't she? She's known me most of my life.' He turned to her then, coolly motioning her to sit and eat. 'Starvation isn't one of the punishments I have in mind for you——'

'Will you stop this absurdity,' Gemma burst out, 'and will you tell me what all this is about? I came here to paint a portrait but so far I've received nothing but abuse.' Her outburst did nothing to ease the scowl on his face. 'You live here, don't you?' she breathed when he said nothing.

'Some of the time, yes.'

Shocked, Gemma slumped into the nearest chair. The familiarity between him and Maria had spurred the question but actually hearing it verified didn't make it any easier to accept, in fact it made it worse. She recalled he had an apartment in New York and another home in South America but because of his Colombian ancestry she had presumed his home was there, not here in Venezuela.

'This . . . this isn't the home of Agustín Delgado de Navas?' she husked. What cruelty! She'd had such expectations and now this rapier-like thrust to add more sorrow to what she had already suffered.

The smile he gave her did nothing to warm his harsh features and chilled Gemma to the marrow.

'He lives here, of course. And you do have his portrait to paint, which no doubt answers your next question. It was my idea, in fact. I convinced Agustín his portrait was necessary. It took some doing, I assure you. He has little time for such eccentricities, as he put it. The idea of a female portrait painter didn't appeal to him much either.'

'Great, that's all I need,' Gemma huffed, bitterness pushing aside her confusion. 'You threatening revenge and torture and a chauvinist who doesn't want his portrait painted. It's nice to know you're wanted!'

Felipe smiled cynically. 'Oh, you are wanted, my love. The revenge and torture will have its moments of hedonism, I promise you. And don't worry about Agustín. I convinced him of your great artistic talent, but kept your others to myself. You have a number of talents, Gemma, bed being one of them, and rest assured I'll put all of them to the test while you are here.'

'You expect me to go to bed with you?' she whispered in disbelief. Once his sexual honesty had excited her; now his presumptuousness struck hard and cold inside her.

'I don't expect it, I demand it, when and where I please.' He took a step towards her and Gemma tensed as his hand smoothed down her cheek while she gazed up at him. Months ago that caress would have inflamed her senses instantly, but now it merely inflamed her anger. She jerked her head away from his touch.

'Am I so abhorrent to you?' He smiled, coldly. 'Not for long, *querida*; lust like ours doesn't dim with time. I'll have you begging for it before I've finished with you.'

Maria stepped back on to the patio with Felipe's brandy and Gemma stilled her fury till she had gone. Felipe sat down at the table across from her and swirled his brandy before swallowing it in a single draught.

Gemma forced a wan smile to her lips. 'Needed that, did you? You'll be a raging alcoholic before I'd consider begging you for the sex you think I so desperately need.'

A genuine smile slicked his face then. 'This is the Gemma Soames I know nothing about—such biting hypocrisy. I like it. It makes a change from the simpering compliance I generally run up against in women.' He shrugged his shoulders dismissively. 'It makes no difference, just adds spice to an otherwise racing certainty.'

'Well, I'd hedge your bets if I were you. I'm not the woman you seduced so easily six months ago——'

'And it was easy, wasn't it?' he cut in cruelly.

Gemma steeled herself, and somehow found the strength to fight him his way—dirty. 'Very,' she parried. 'It didn't take much to get *you* into bed either, did it?'

His fists bunched on the wrought-iron arm of his chair and his eyes blazed angrily. 'Don't talk that way, like a whore!'

Gemma held his eyes, fighting the whiplash of the insult. Suddenly she wasn't afraid of him any more, not afraid to hurt him either because this wasn't the man she had loved so passionately and wouldn't have dreamed of hurting for all the world six months ago. This man was a cruel, heartless stranger.

'It's all right for you to insult me, though, isn't it?' She sighed theatrically. 'But of course this is South America, not St John's Wood, and here women do as they're told, so you tell me.'

'Because they want to. They love their men enough to bow to their every wish.'

'How very quaintly old-fashioned. The women's movement would have a field day down here.'

'They'd get nowhere.'

'You're probably right,' sighed Gemma. 'I'm not interested enough to argue with you.'

'And your complacency was the reason you didn't call me in New York?' he accused bitingly.

There was a long pause before Gemma could answer. Surely that wasn't what all this was about, a wretched phone call that was never made?

'Did you really expect that I would?' she answered bleakly. Had he honestly expected her to go running after him after what he had done to her?

'I should have known. Your sort of women want it all one way—their own. You took what you wanted from me and cast me aside for the next acquisition. Many no doubt in the circles you mix in.'

There was no room for hurt when indignation rose in her throat. 'Is that why you came to my exhibition, to pick up the sort of woman you expected would frequent such a place? I thought exhibitions were for the purpose of viewing art, not trawling for loose women. My mistake again, as everything seems to be my mistake where you are concerned.'

'You haven't eaten,' he said, nodding to the food in front of her.

Very revealing, thought Gemma. Point out a few home truths and a change of subject is always worth a try.

She pushed the plate away. 'After your brutality I have no appetite,' she told him. 'How's Bianca, by the way?' she asked sarcastically, adding her own slice of brutality, though it was hurting her more than him, she realised as soon as she said it.

His eyes pierced hers and a muscle at his jawline tightened threateningly. 'She's well and will be here next week, so you will see for yourself,' he told her cruelly.

Can't wait, Gemma murmured inwardly, and reached for the jug of orange juice Maria had left. She couldn't eat—his cruelty drove hunger from her—but fluids were essential. The heat was making her feel very light-headed—or was it the thought that Bianca's arriving next week was engineered by Felipe to add insult to the injury he was already inflicting on her?

'Why did you bring me here?' she asked after slaking her thirst.

'Because I was bored with making love to you in my mind. I wanted you in the flesh. I couldn't live another day without possessing you for real.'

Gemma gazed at him painfully. He made making love sound as if it only meant sex. Was that how he had seen their affair? He'd said a thousand times that he had loved her, and, gullible as she had been, she had believed him. Not now, though. He wanted to punish her, drive her to the edge of desire and then spurn her as he thought she had done to him and that was spiteful and cruel and was aeons away from the caring he had shown before.

'To punish me, or for your own pleasure?' she asked levelly.

'Both. I hate myself as much as you for what happened in London.' He smiled cynically at her. 'Trouble is, I still desire you, and you know the best cure for an obsession, don't you? Face it. Over and over again till you exorcise it from your life.'

'You hate me that much,' Gemma breathed sadly, 'and all because I didn't phone you?' She drew in a ragged breath, still not able to fully understand. 'Felipe, I didn't call you because you walked out of my life as easily as you walked into it——'

'I had reason to, but you didn't give me a chance——'

'Should I have done? The call came a week later! Why not sooner?' She shook her head miserably. 'I don't know why I'm bothering arguing with you. It makes no difference now.' She stood up and looked across at him. 'I did love you, Felipe, and I thank you for bringing me here. You've exorcised any ghosts I had spooking around after you left me. If you want help to get me out of your system, go summon a psychiatrist; no way are you going to do it by taking me to bed, how and when you please.'

He stood up and faced her, anger darkening his face. 'I might not need to stoop so low,' he grated, 'because I'm seeing you in a new light. What happened to the soft, sweet Gemma I fell in love with?'

'She got hurt, Felipe. So now we both know how it feels.' She tilted her chin defiantly. 'You can't hurt me any more than you already have. I dare say with your expertise you could tempt me into your bed, but for what? Sex, no more, no less. It could never be anything else for me, Felipe, never!'

How easily the lies slid from her tongue. Sex: it had
never been just that, and it wouldn't be if ever he did
manipulate her into his bed again. She had truly loved
him and yet now she wanted to hurt him as he was
hurting her, and suddenly she didn't care that she was
cheapening herself in his eyes.

'You talk like a bitch!' he breathed.

'If you say so, so be it,' she conceded frostily, and
turned away from him.

He didn't follow her, and Gemma went straight
back into the house the way she had come out, round
the side of the villa to the front. There were tears of
fury and pain in her eyes but she willed them away,
at least till she got to her room. The house was
blessedly cool, and, sweeping her hair from the heat
of her face, she started to climb the stairs.

'*Señorita*, you don't like the food I prepare for
you?'

Gemma swung round and looked down at the hurt
expression in Maria's eyes as she stood in the hallway.
For a few seconds she was dazed by the statement and
then she understood.

'No, Maria, it wasn't that. I'm just too hot and
tired to eat at the moment. I'm sorry you went to the
trouble.'

She wished she'd eaten, not for her own sake but
Maria's. It was mid-afternoon and probably the
custom here, as in most hot countries, to take siesta.
Maria had gone out of her way to prepare food for
her when she should have been resting.

'It's no trouble. You eat with Felipe later, *si*?'

'No!' Her retort came too quickly and Maria
frowned. Gemma smiled and softened her voice. 'I
want to rest and . . . and . . .' And what? She needed

space and time to think, that was what. Somehow she had to get out of this hateful predicament.

'*Si*, I understand,' grinned Maria. 'Later I bring you food.' She ambled away into the shadowy depths of a corridor. Relieved, Gemma ran up the rest of the stairs to her room.

She stripped off her clothes, showered, wrapped herself in a towel and slumped on the bed. Her head ached miserably from the heated exchange between her and Felipe. He'd said it all in that brief but painful altercation. This was a Gemma Soames he knew nothing about. But was it any wonder? Once she had been happy and carefree, but lately she had been morose and bitter, and it was all his fault.

How very little they did know of each other. They were familiar with each other's bodies but that was all. She would never have believed him capable of such cruelty. The very idea of him bringing her here to make her suffer was quite astonishing. He believed she had rejected him, his Hispanic descent had taken that as a personal humiliation and now he was determined to humiliate her in return.

Gemma buried her face in the cool lace bedspread. She felt sick and weary and wished with all her heart she had listened to her mother and not taken this assignment.

When she finally raised herself out of a deep sleep it was dark. Amber candle lights glowed softly in wrought-iron fixtures on the wall. The fan above the bed whirred softly. For a second Gemma wasn't sure where she was and then it all folded over her, a black cloud of depression.

She got up, splashed her face with water, and found her white satin robe hanging on the back of the bathroom door, freshly ironed.

She slid into it and found that Maria had unpacked for her, ironed all her clothes and put them away.

'You are awake,' Maria said as she stepped softly into the room. 'Felipe would like you to go down for dinner but he said not to worry if you have the lag jet.'

Such thoughtfulness from Felipe would have gone unnoticed before, but now it throbbed with suspicion. But maybe he'd had time to think how unreasonable he had been.

'I feel a little better, Maria, but not enough to dress and go down for dinner. Is Señor de Navas back yet?'

'No, not for a few days yet,' Maria told her, straightening the bedspread.

Pity, thought Gemma, she would have made the effort for him, her father. The thought didn't excite her any more, just speared regret through her. She shouldn't have come.

So she had a few days to kill before he came back. Under any other circumstances she would have welcomed the wait. It would give her the chance to fully recover from her 'lag jet' and emotionally prepare her for coming face to face with her real father. Now, with Felipe around to torment her, the waiting could be doubly insufferable. Depression washed over her in a fresh wave of despair.

'Señorita...' Maria started, but suddenly she became tongue-tied and a slight flush rose to her cheeks.

'Please call me Gemma,' Gemma said, trying to put her at her ease.

Maria smiled, 'Gemma,' she repeated, having difficulty with the soft G, and it came out as if she had something stuck in the back of her throat. 'Felipe, he tell me why you are here...'

Gemma froze, her hand suspended over her head as she was brushing her hair. Surely he hadn't confided in the housekeeper, told her they had been lovers and the reason he had engineered this commission?

'Is my daughter, Christina. She love the Americano and he one day go back home and maybe he take my daughter with him... she is all I have. Maybe... you have time to do a... to do a small picture...' Suddenly she shook her head. 'No, I should not ask...'

Gemma grinned, half with relief, half with pleasure. 'Oh, Maria, you want me to paint your daughter?'

Maria shook her head again, twisted her hands in front of her. 'I should not ask...'

'I'd love to do it,' Gemma laughed with relief. It was a marvellous idea. It would keep her occupied and soothe her ravaged thoughts and how could she refuse such a heart-rending request?

'I pay,' Maria smiled, relief flooding her motherly features.

'You won't!' Gemma protested. 'It will be a gift from me to you. It will be a pleasure to do it,' she told the woman, lightly squeezing her arm to prove she meant it.

Flushed with pleasure Maria turned away and stopped at the door. 'I bring you food. You must eat and I tell Christina. She will be much excited.'

Gemma finished brushing her hair and wished she could brush away the depression with it. Well, at least, that was one problem solved—what to do with herself while she waited for Agustín de Navas. Would Felipe mind? She presumed that Maria's daughter also worked here but there was no reason why the girl couldn't sit for her in her spare time. But what had it to do with Felipe anyway—this was Agustín's home, wasn't it? But Felipe lived here and Maria addressed him as if he was the head of the household in Agustín's absence.

She frowned in bewilderment as she lay her brush down on the dressing table. Why did Felipe live here anyway? True, only some of the time, but he was here now, none the less. She knew he had something to do with finance in the oil-field sector. Was he an adviser to her father... to Agustín? The remoteness of the sprawling hacienda would warrant a long stay if Agustín operated his empire from home. But that was only a presumption. The truth she longed to know but would it make any difference to the terrible predicament she found herself in?

The blackness outside her bedroom window gave no answers as she stared bleakly out, holding back the drapes with one hand. Strange how life twisted and turned, forever catching you unawares. She had come out here with trepidation in her heart at the thought of coming face to face with the man who was her father. Now that trepidation was for another man, her one-time lover, Felipe Santos. The fear of what he had in mind for her now outweighed the apprehension she felt at meeting Agustín de Navas.

'I'm sorry you don't feel well enough to join me downstairs for dinner. The mountain comes to Mahomet, as you probably intended.'

His voice was raw with sarcasm and Gemma swung to face him.

'That *wasn't* the intention.' She scowled as he put a tray of food down on one of the sideboards. 'I'm not playing games as you suppose. I could hardly anticipate your doing such a menial task as bringing my dinner up, could I?'

'Nothing surprises me about you. You're sharp enough to realise that I would be annoyed by your stubbornness and not let it pass.'

'I was under the impression I had a choice—to join you downstairs or to eat in my room,' Gemma retorted. 'In fact, I thought how considerate you were to think I might be suffering from jet lag. How wrong I was.'

'*Are* you suffering from the after-effects of your long journey?' He smiled coldly, his deep-set eyes sweeping over the provocative white satin of her robe.

Gemma stood her ground, not rising to the giveaway action of tightening it around her in an attempt at propriety. He knew what lay beneath it well enough.

'Aren't I allowed even that small weakness?' she asked bitterly.

'Only if I'm allowed one too.'

Because she wasn't expecting it, her body wasn't geared for defence. His hand shot out and slid round her waist and in one swift thrust she was hauled hard against him. His mouth was hot on hers, hot, demanding and deadly in the instant desire it sprang in her. His tongue eased past her lips, grazed heatedly over the soft inner skin of her lips, numbing her senses to why he was doing this.

A noise came from his throat, animal-like, predatory, uncontrollable. It was one she recognised and had always thrilled to in the past. An admission from him that the power of his love demanded her complete surrender, here and now and with an urgency that left her breathless. She had always matched his eagerness with a depth of desire that never ceased to arouse him to the limits of his endurance.

It was happening now, that turbulent flush of emotions coursing through her that had her aching so intensely for his penetration. His hand now sliding over the soft satin, now kneading her flesh beneath it till the white heat of desire scorched every negative pulse under her skin as if a virulent flame had flash-fired over her body.

Her mind spun with the depth of the need, and so intense was it that she couldn't register that this was just a punishment, his revenge, his torment. His hands, burning now, hard with intention, thrust beyond the thin fabric, scored across her breasts, drawing a deep gasp from Gemma's throat.

He held her breast fiercely to guide her aroused nipple to his mouth, drew deeply on it as if he was sampling some rare, sweet wine and wanted to savour the very last drop.

Gemma's hands flew to his hair, twisting the familiar springy silken coils in her fevered fingers, holding him against her for fear of losing him again.

But he was lost, her tormented senses reasoned. He hated her. Believed she had wronged him and not the other way around. This was the torment he had promised her. But surely he must be in pain too? Surely this wasn't an act put on for the purpose of revenge? He needed her, desperately. The hardness of his body thrusting against the heat of her own, the breath quickening in his throat, his moist mouth so possessive and demanding on her breasts, couldn't be faked.

And then it was all over, the desire swept away on a swirling current of painful memories of betrayal. Their thoughts and reasoning coupled as their bodies weren't going to be allowed to.

They both drew back from each other at the same instant and their glazed eyes locked painfully.

'Hardly the way I had anticipated it ending,' he grated harshly, pulling her robe around her and tightening the belt viciously.

Gemma clasped her shoulders and hugged herself for some sort of comfort. Her body trembled under the satin, not with desire but with the shock of the cold cessation of his embrace.

'I . . . I thought that was the whole point of the exercise,' Gemma whispered in a voice roughened by the intensity of her confused feelings. She knew in that moment that she wanted him as much as she ever had, not a need fuelled by just wanting his body but a need fuelled by love. She hadn't been wrong about her feelings for him and a week had been long enough to prove that it was real. Her love was all still there, badly tarnished by his cruelty, but nevertheless there, deep in her heart. The confusion came for him. Didn't he realise that too, that they had had something special and that whatever had passed could be resolved?

'You'd better eat before your food gets cold,' he said brittly, turning away from her and stopping at the door.

It wasn't what she wanted to hear, this abrupt change of subject once again. She wanted him to tackle her, she wanted a blazing row because sometimes good came out of such furious confrontations. But he had stopped and he was facing her and he had something more to say. She held her breath, absurdly anticipating and wishing something harsh and cruel to come from his beautiful mouth, an insult she could match and thrust back at him to start the ball rolling.

'Tomorrow, after you are fully rested, I'll show you over the rest of the hacienda. You'll find enough to occupy yourself with till Agustín returns.'

'I already have something to do,' she blurted, ridiculously hoping that he would object to her intermediary commission and so start the row she so longed for. 'Maria asked me if I would do a painting of Christina for her.'

Her heart raced as his brow darkened. 'She shouldn't have done that,' he said tightly. 'I'll have a word with her.'

'No!' Gemma cried, clenching her fists at her side. That hadn't been her intention, to get Maria into trouble. She'd handled it all wrong and now Maria was going to be on the receiving end of his wrath, not her.

His eyes narrowed at her protest and his fingers whitened on the edge of the door.

'No,' Gemma repeated. 'She was hesitant about asking me, said she shouldn't have, but Christina is all she has and...and she wanted something to remember her by if...if one day she decided to go away.'

She didn't mention Mike. He might not know that Agustín's pilot was in love with Maria's daughter. She was walking a tightrope for Maria as it was.

'She kindly offered to pay, but I said I would do it for nothing. It will keep me busy while I'm waiting.

I don't know what Christina's position is in the household, but I promise I won't let it interfere with her duties.'

Suddenly she didn't want the row she had been needling for. It had all gone wrong and he wasn't angry with her any more but with Maria, and that wasn't fair.

'She has enough spare time, so I don't think it will be a problem,' he said quietly, and relief flooded Gemma. 'At least it will keep you out of my hair,' he added brutally. 'Give you time to reflect on what nearly happened in this room tonight. Don't think for a minute that I've eased up on you, Gemma. Making love to you tonight doesn't fit into my plans. But when I'm good and ready for you, you'll know. I'll have you hammering on my bedroom door before very long.'

All hope faded and Gemma tensed the body that only minutes before had melted in his arms like butter in the sun.

'Sure you will,' she conceded, braving a cynical smile. 'I'll be hammering on your door with a feather and I won't have to do it twice, will I? Because you'll be waiting eagerly enough, and you won't have torment on your mind, will you?'

She thought that his rage would burst out and he'd murder her there and then and put them both out of their misery. His face darkened thunderously, his grip tightened so fiercely on the door that she feared he'd rip it from its iron brackets. But this was a new Felipe, one she was so terribly unsure of, one who didn't do what she expected of him.

'Sleep well, *querida*,' he said, controlled and immobile now. 'Think on what I have said and prepare yourself for the onslaught. It's not a threat but a promise.'

He closed the door infuriatingly softly behind him and Gemma stemmed a cry of frustration in her throat.

CHAPTER THREE

GEMMA was up early the next morning. She'd slept enough for a month and awoken refreshed, though as soon as her feet touched the rug by the bed Felipe's threats swamped her once again.

She wasn't going to let it weigh her down, though, she determined. That was what he wanted: to undermine her confidence till she was an emotional wreck. She was halfway there, she suspected, but no one was going to know it.

After showering she dressed in a cool lemon sundress with thin shoulder straps and slipped on soft leather flip-flops. She grabbed her Ray-Ban sunglasses as she went out of the room. Her eyes ached this morning, a reminder that she wasn't as brave as she was trying to be. She'd fought tears last night, battled with them till her eyes ached so badly that she had been tempted to give in and let them flow. But she wouldn't give him an inch, let alone her tears!

The villa was still and Gemma hoped she was first up, hoped that no one would mind if she got her bearings in the old villa.

She paused on the stone stairway to study the paintings. Nothing she recognised, like a Renoir, a Turner or a Picasso. Mostly old portraits of the family, handed down from generation to generation. She wondered if any were of Agustín but saw none that had been painted in the last fifty years. There were no portraits of women, she noted, but wasn't sur-

prised. This was a macho country where the women
didn't count for much, she cynically supposed.

The downstairs rooms were cool and airy. Huge
rooms with high ceilings, heavily beamed, white-
washed stone walls and polished terracotta floor tiles
throughout. The furnishings were in keeping with the
villa, heavy antiques of dark carved wood. Tapestries
of ancient hunting scenes decorated the walls and the
sprawling sofas were upholstered in luxurious bro-
cades. The Hereke rugs on the tiles were flat woven
in shades of blue, red and ivory with flashes of gilded
thread. Real gold? Gemma wondered.

There were bowls of flowers everywhere, roses to
scent the air, lilies and the exotic orchids that decorated her own bedroom. The house, though sombre,
was very beautiful, and a peculiar thought struck
Gemma—that no children had exploded with laughter
within these walls. In fact it had the awesome feel of
a museum where children were inhibited and silent.

One room was locked and Gemma presumed that
to be Agustín's private domain, his study possibly.
Running out of rooms, she followed the corridor to
the kitchen. She opened a door at the end, a heavy
studded affair similar to all the doors in the house
but this one somewhat newer.

This was where the heart of the home pulsed. The
kitchen was huge, bright and a century more modern
than anything she had seen so far.

Maria turned from the huge stainless steel range
where she was frying crisp bacon and turning round
flat pancakes in a pan. The smell was delicious and
cheered Gemma, which made her reflect that though
the rest of the house was beautiful it had slightly de-
pressed her.

'Gemma, you are well, *si*? Felipe is with the horses.'

Gemma could see for herself. She saw him through the open door at the back of the kitchen. He was exercising a black stallion in the paddock in front of the stables. He wore a black T-shirt with white riding breeches and even from this distance she could see that the gauntness she had first noticed about him was confined to his face, not his body. He was still a muscular, powerful man, but the hunted look gave the impression of an overall weight loss.

Her heart ached to think she might be the cause, but surely not? He hated her now, didn't he? But the torment he had promised her was giving him no satisfaction. This revenge that was powering him was doing more harm than good.

Gemma turned away from the door as Maria called her for breakfast, an informal affair round an oak refectory table, which reminded Gemma that she was here for a purpose, to work—she wasn't a guest in the house.

'Christina cleans the bedrooms and will be finished soon. You start the picture then?' Maria asked eagerly as Gemma ate her breakfast.

'Later, Maria,' came a voice from the back door, and Gemma turned her head to look at Felipe. He stood framed in the doorway, the glaring light of the day behind him silhouetting him as if he were the devil himself taking a day out from hell.

'I wish to spend the morning with Gemma. Christina can sit for her this afternoon.' He sat across the table from her and laid his riding crop down on the bench seat next to him as if he might need it at any moment.

Gemma mentally slapped herself. She was becoming paranoid with the thoughts of the torture he had predicted for her.

'You slept well?' he asked, concentrating on the enormous breakfast of bacon, eggs and pancakes Maria set down in front of him.

'Yes, thank you,' she answered politely, lifting her coffee-cup to her lips and watching him over the rim. 'I thought I was an early riser but you beat me to it. I saw you exercising your horse.'

'A gentle exercise. I breed racehorses. Tomorrow he goes to stud and needs his strength. Would you like to watch?' There was a glint of cynical humour in his dark eyes at the suggestion and an apprehensive Gemma saw it as another cut and thrust.

'No, thank you,' Gemma said primly, lowering her lashes in embarrassment.

'Perhaps you would like to see the teaser stallion at work, then. Not quite so stimulating but very necessary and interesting none the less.'

'Teaser stallion?' Gemma breathed cautiously, her curiosity reluctantly aroused.

'A teaser stallion is introduced to the mare to get the heavy business of courtship over before the sire takes the final glory. If the teaser tries to mount the mare, she's ready, then the breeding stallion is brought in.'

'That's awful!' Gemma protested. 'It's not fair.'

'There's not much fair in love and war,' he said meaningfully.

Gemma ignored the indication and retorted, 'Tell that to the poor teaser!'

'Oh, they have their moments,' he told her, refilling his coffee-cup. 'Haven't you heard the story of

Archive, a not very successful racehorse who was demoted from the turf to life as a teaser? Bright Cherry fell in love with him and wanted only him, continually spurned her classier intended. Her owner sympathised and eventually let her have her own way. The foal that came out of that illicit union was Arkle, one of the greatest steeplechasers of all times.'

Gemma smiled, reluctantly. 'That sounds like a shaggy horse story, if you ask me.'

'It's true, I promise you,' Felipe told her convincingly.

Gemma let the smile fade from her lips. Maybe there was a warning disguised in that tale too. Maybe Bianca was the female counterpart of a teaser, being brought in as part of Felipe's plan to torment her, to drive her into his arms so that he could spurn her. But wasn't it more likely he simply wanted Bianca here for himself, in which case she, Gemma, might turn out to be the teaser in Bianca's eyes!

'Are you ready for your tour of inspection?' Felipe asked, pushing his breakfast plate away.

'Yes, but first can I see where I'm expected to paint the portrait? Did you order everything I asked for?' She could hardly believe her own voice, behaving as if everything was perfectly normal between them.

Felipe picked her sunglasses up from the table and handed them to her as they got up. Their fingers brushed and their eyes locked for a second. Both looked away at the same time.

'It wasn't necessary to order everything on the list. The canvases, yes, but there is a fully equipped studio here.'

The shades over her eyes concealed her look of surprise as they stepped outside.

'Who's the artist, then?' she asked. She still knew nothing about the man she was going to paint. She'd seen no evidence of a wife or children of Agustín's, though like her they would probably be grown up now and have fled the nest. So who was the artist: Agustín himself?

'No one,' Felipe told her tightly as they strolled through the rose gardens towards the pool.

Gemma didn't press him. Maybe the studio was a whim of a rich man, one who had so much money he didn't know what to splash out on next. It was a bonus for Gemma, though; she'd been worried about where she was going to work. She'd seen nowhere suitable to set up her canvas in her foray this morning. Only the kitchen had sufficient light and she could hardly picture the wealthy oil baron posing with a backdrop of culinary paraphernalia.

'Do you swim?' Felipe asked as they paused on the terrace overlooking the pool.

It was a stunning pool, circular, blue, cool and inviting. A fountain splashed gently in the centre surrounded by natural stone. The water cascaded down the rock and back into the pool. Gemma was mesmerised by the light spinning off the tumbling water, shafting tiny rainbows around the fountain. She tore her eyes away to look at Felipe. Her heart ached to think he didn't even know she could swim; it ached to think she didn't know if he could either. But thoughts like that were non-productive. He was being passably reasonable to her at the moment and she owed him some effort of her own.

'Yes, I'm no dolphin but I love the water,' she murmured.

'Good, then later we will bathe. Do you ride?'

'Definitely not,' Gemma told him with a grin. 'Anything bigger than a Shetland pony terrifies me.'

Felipe laughed but didn't suggest he teach her. She was grateful for that small mercy.

They strolled round the pool and through an archway of crimson bougainvillaea to a part of the garden that took Gemma's breath away. It was shaded by fronds of sun-wilted cane but what hung beneath in rows and racks raised up from the ground was a delight to the eye. Orchids, hundreds of them, waxy, exotic, colourful. They trailed from tubs and baskets, thick and heavy with blooms.

'They are beautiful, quite fantastic!' Gemma breathed.

Felipe broke off a flower, creamy white and slightly trumpet-shaped, so perfect it would have cost a mint if boxed and offered for sale in London or Paris. He smiled and tucked it behind Gemma's ear, arranging her thick silken mane of jet hair around it to hold it in place.

Gemma couldn't hold his eyes. She was distressed and yet puzzled by the pain in his, and fearful of the touch of his fingers lightly brushing against her cheek.

She turned away, not really understanding that look. She pretended to study one of the more unusual blooms. She heard him emit a small laugh behind her and then she understood. It was all a game to him, she thought bitterly, a very cruel one at that. Well, she wouldn't toss the flower crossly aside. He would expect that and he'd know he'd got to her.

'Are they yours?' she asked.

'Mine and Agustín's. A hobby we share.'

Gemma frowned. She wanted to know more but Felipe had already turned away and was heading back to the pool area. She caught him up.

'Do you work for him?' Another question that shouldn't need to be asked. After the intensity of their affair she should know everything about him but sadly she didn't.

'Yes. I'm his financial director.'

Gemma wanted even more. 'Can you tell me a bit about him? I mean . . . it's necessary for my work. I need to know what sort of man he is if the portrait is to be a success.'

'He can be a bastard,' Felipe told her flatly, without looking at her. 'But he's wealthy and successful and that usually impresses most women.'

Was that a dig that she was one of 'most women'? She let it pass and explored the idea of painting a rich, successful bastard who happened to be her father.

They were beyond the pool now and heading towards the tiny church close to the villa. Gemma hadn't noticed before but there was a covered walkway from double doors at the side of the villa to the church. A quick mental calculation worked out that the double doors came from the locked room, Agustín de Navas's private study. Was he a religious man? The church was almost on the doorstep.

'This is where you will work—providing, of course, Agustín approves. The place has been shut up for years.' Felipe plunged his hand into his pocket for a key.

Gemma was about to protest that no way was she going to paint a portrait in a house of worship, unless

it was of a bishop or the Pope, when Felipe threw
open the door.

He went ahead of her to swing back the drapes at
the windows. Gemma took off her sunglasses, dis-
lodged the orchid from behind her ear and it fell to
the ground. She stooped to retrieve it and when she
straightened up drew in a sharp breath.

The church wasn't a church at all but the most
beautiful studio she had ever seen. The ceiling was
vaulted, giving the impression of the shape of a church
from outside. The floor was golden polished pine
though dusty and dirty with neglect.

There were several windows and Felipe was busy
casting the dusty drapes aside, filling the spacious
room with motes that danced in the sun-streaked air.

The last window was huge, almost from floor to
ceiling, and Felipe released the blind that covered it.
Light flooded the room, not bright sunlight because
the area outside was shaded by trees, but a diffused
light that was just perfect to work by.

Gemma wandered around in awe, this unexpected
bonus for a moment casting away her troubles. There
was a small kitchen screened off by an Oriental screen
of bamboo and a door to a tiny bathroom with a toilet
and shower cubicle. There were several easels leaning
against the white walls and there were couches of dusty
slubbed silk dotted around. The open shelves on one
wall were stocked with jugs of brushes, pots of paint,
tins of pastels, pencils, charcoal. Mounted canvases
of every shape and size were stacked neatly in one
corner.

'None of this has ever been used,' Gemma said,
turning to Felipe, her eyes wide with puzzlement.

'It will be now,' Felipe told her, his voice echoing slightly in the high ceilinged studio. 'I'll get the women in to clean it. It's about time the place saw the light of day.'

'But what is it here for if no one ever uses it?'

Felipe didn't answer straight away, but ran his fingers over the back of a hard-backed chair and examined the dirt on his fingers.

'Felipe?' Gemma husked.

His eyes met hers at last, dark and impenetrable. 'Rumour has it he had it built for a woman, someone he met in Europe, someone he cared deeply for long ago...'

Gemma felt the floor tilt under her and she grasped the back of one of the couches she was standing by. Oh, God, had Agustín built this place for her mother?

'Though it's hard to imagine Agustín caring deeply for anyone,' Felipe went on flintily, 'least of all his long-suffering wife.'

His wife? There was such bitterness in his tone that it added to Gemma's sickness. She edged her way round the couch. She had to sit down before she collapsed. So Agustín was married. She had hoped he wasn't. A wife was an added complication to her already overloaded emotions.

'His...his wife?' she breathed.

'She died a few years ago. Blessed release for her, in my opinion. It wasn't a happy marriage.'

'Why didn't they divorce?' Gemma asked heavily.

'Divorce?' Felipe snapped disdainfully. 'You forget, this is a Catholic country. Marriage is for life.'

'And you have to make the best of it if it all goes wrong,' Gemma mused out loud.

'It's better to be sure you have the right woman in the first place,' Felipe uttered evenly, as if it were all as simple as that.

Gemma looked up at him, hoping to read something in that remark, but there was nothing. Marriage had never been spoken of during their affair in London, but how could it have been? A week was nothing in their relationship and yet they had felt so deeply for each other that surely marriage would have been the inevitable conclusion? Perhaps, but then Bianca had come between them.

'What's wrong?' Felipe leaned across the couch and smoothed her hair from her cheeks. 'You look pale.' His voice was almost tender. Gemma was on alert.

She forced a hesitant smile to her lips. Just the thought of that woman with Felipe drained the blood from her cheeks.

'I'm OK—the heat maybe. It's so stuffy in here.' She composed herself, quickly, concentrated her thoughts away from him and Bianca. 'You . . . you paint such a black picture of Agustín.'

Felipe straightened up. 'Do I? He's a complex man. He runs his empire with a rod of iron and doesn't ease up in his personal life. He's arrogant, proud and can be abominably objectionable . . .'

Sounds just like you, Gemma nearly retorted.

' . . . and painting his portrait should prove to be a bundle of fun for you.'

'Another form of punishment for me?' Gemma asked, suddenly feeling thoroughly miserable about everything. She hadn't wanted a saint as a father, but this man sounded positively hellish.

Felipe suddenly smiled, the warmth getting as far as his eyes. 'No, my sweet,' he said softly. 'Just an unfortunate truth that has little to do with me this time. Come, let's get out of here. This place is like a bloody mausoleum!'

Or more like a shrine, Gemma thought morbidly.

'Could you face a swim before lunch?' he asked gently.

Such thoughtfulness. Warily, Gemma turned the power of her thoughts in that direction rather than towards Agustín, his wife, and her mother. Later, when she was alone, she would spare some thought to Felipe's revelations but now she needed her wits about her. Felipe was being too nice and an about-turn was inevitable. She wanted to be alert and ready for it.

'Yes, I'd like that very much,' she replied.

After her initial shyness at posing for Gemma, Christina settled and sat very still on a chair by the window. Maria hovered in the background, making out she was baking, but not much was going in or coming out of the oven, Gemma thought with amusement.

Gemma started work with a very rapid, rough outline in white on one of the smaller canvases she'd taken from the studio, asking Felipe's permission first. It was going to be easy; Christina had an interesting face. She was beautiful, which helped; but there was more. Christina was in love and it showed. She had a certain serenity that softened her very black eyes, added a sheen to her olive skin and a fullness to her lips.

Gemma tried not to think of affairs such as love as she worked, but it was as impossible as damming a flood-swollen river.

Where was the torment Felipe had promised her? She'd seen only a hint of it this day. As they lay sprawled in the sun after their swim she had opened her eyes and caught his eyes on her body. She had covered herself soon after, using the intensity of the sun's rays as an excuse. Truth was, the look had painfully reminded her of his tireless exploration of her body when they had been in love. Then he had worshipped and cosseted her body, but now he was punishing her and she felt the threat through his ravaging eyes. Bravely she had fought the wave of arousal that came with his perusal. It wouldn't do to show a sign of weakness to him.

'Rest, Christina,' Gemma said, cleaning her brush with a rag and stepping back from the easel to study her work. She had explained to Maria that she wouldn't have time for a full portrait, just a head and shoulders with no background. Now they both crowded round and Gemma laughed at the disappointed expressions on both their faces.

'I know it doesn't look much now, but I promise you you'll like it when it's finished,' she told them.

It was a very satisfying afternoon, Gemma had to admit, with the three women laughing and chatting. Gemma forced aside thoughts of Felipe and threw herself into her work. She loved encouraging her subjects to chat as they sat. It relaxed the model and was so important to Gemma to catch just the right character of a person. She remembered Felipe's commenting on the industrialist she had painted and how boring and pompous he looked. She couldn't have painted him any other way because that was the man. She couldn't have spun her thoughts away from Felipe if she tried, either, she had to concede finally. He was there all the time, hovering on the periphery of her sanity, just waiting to tip her over the edge.

'Well, you've started, and a much more charming subject than that industrialist,' Felipe said behind her as she worked, his voice low, intended for her ears only.

It shocked her that she was thinking of the very same man at that moment. It hurt too. Reminded her of the times when it had happened before. Both spoken of the same subject at the same time and both collapsed with laughter at the coincidence.

'Funny, I was just thinking of the man at that very moment you spoke of him,' she said quietly, almost remorsefully.

'And were you also thinking of what followed that night?' he whispered, so derisively that Gemma tensed.

She recovered quickly. She was forgetting, this was all part of the highs and lows of the torment game.

'That's enough for today, Christina.' Ignoring Felipe's remark, she gathered up her brushes from the table and crossed to the sink to clean them.

Christina and Maria gathered round the small canvas again and Gemma only half listened to their cries of pleasure. She was swamped with hurt, a hurt she must keep from her tormentor at all costs. He wasn't going to win.

He joined her at the sink, stood so close to her his body heat seared her skin.

'That stung, did it?'

'What?' she said glibly. She wasn't going to give him the satisfaction of knowing she'd been hurt.

'Don't act so dumb. You know what I mean.'

'I do,' she sighed reluctantly, 'but you're wasting your time, Felipe. I don't object to you winding me up, you can't hurt me any more,' she lied, 'but not in front of the staff, eh? That shows your weakness, not mine.'

'The staff know their place, which is more than can be said for you, sweet one. And when it comes down to weakness, we'll soon see who survives this test.' He poured two coffees.

Numbly, Gemma waited till Maria and Christina left the room before challenging him.

'Torment is the test, is it? You're wasting your time and mine,' she told him strongly. 'You make me feel like the week's washing hurtling through the hot cycle of a washing machine. Cold fill, heat to ninety degrees, swoosh around for half an hour, finish off with a dousing of cold again and a fast spin.' She shrugged her shoulders and smiled at him. 'It's a complete waste of time because next week you'll have to put me through the whole process again. I'm like a pair of Marks and Spencer's knickers: I'll never wear out.'

'Indestructible, are you?' he smiled cynically, spooning sugar into her cup for her. 'We'll see about that.'

Gemma frowned. 'Why, Felipe? You think you're hurting me but you're hurting yourself as much. It's like some sort of self-abuse. What you're doing isn't a characteristic I admire in a man.'

'And cold, calculated rejection isn't something I admire in a woman,' he returned bluntly, handing her a cup of coffee.

Gemma took it and leaned back against the sink to drink it.

'I was under the impression I was the rejected one. All the time you have been plotting this misguided revenge of yours I suppose it never occurred to you that I was the injured party.'

'I expected you to phone me in New York——'

'It was too late then. Seven days too late!'

'Your love wasn't strong enough to wait a week?' he challenged sarcastically. 'What sort of love is that?'

Gemma gazed at him painfully. This could never be resolved. His humiliation ran so deep it was unfathomable. She drew a deep breath.

'I went to your house the next day,' she admitted to him in a hoarse whisper. 'You'd gone and so had Bianca. What was I supposed to think?'

'So you went to my house to check up on me? You mistrusted me then?' His eyes were loaded with disgust and Gemma turned hers away from him. It hadn't been like that but convincing him otherwise was a hopeless waste of time.

'I don't expect to answer to you for every movement I make, then or now,' he thrust back at her.

Gemma raised her eyes to his at that. 'No, I don't suppose a macho Latin lover does! Get real, Felipe!'

'I am real, sweet one,' he replied harshly. 'You're the one who's out of line, so damned unreal you live in fantasy land. Do you think I didn't have reason to do what I did? You think after what we had been to each other I would let it slip from my grasp?'

Gemma shook her head in dismay. 'One week, Felipe. We had one week together. Hardly long enough to build any trust...'

'Long enough to fall in love, though,' he challenged. 'Or maybe we were both under the same severe misinterpretation of our actions and the thrashing around we did so successfully wasn't love at all but plain old fornication! And that's phrasing it politely!' he added bitterly.

Pain throbbed in Gemma's veins. It had come to this, had it? They had loved each other, it had been real, but now all they could do was pour acid abuse on each other's already smarting emotions. She knew it but couldn't stop herself adding her own poison.

'And then came Bianca,' Gemma challenged him slowly.

She studied his face intently, with eyes as glacial as his own. Weeks she had wrestled with the idea of him and Bianca being lovers. They were cousins but that wasn't any consolation to Gemma; laws didn't forbid it everywhere. She had seen the look in Bianca's eyes for Felipe and could still recall the hostility she had shown to her. Bianca wanted Felipe, Bianca hated Gemma, Bianca had won.

She felt there was no denial coming, but had she really expected it?

'Yes, and then came Bianca,' he breathed steadily. 'Someone who has been a part of my life a helluva lot longer than you have.'

'In other words, "Shove off Gemma, you've kept my bed warm long enough——"'

His hand shot to her chin and he thumbed her lips punishingly as if scoring her mouth clean. 'You talk like a fishwife and act like a whore——'

'And you would know just how both act, wouldn't you?'

His mouth hard on hers was his answer, proving that the latter part of his insult had something going for it. Her eyes filled with tears beneath her lids. He hated her, could wound her desperately with his in-

sults, but that treacherous desire was already stretching
its tentacles to her reasoning. She *was* a whore if she
couldn't control this rush of need he roused in her
with just one impassioned kiss.

She wrenched her mouth from his, painfully because his teeth grazed her lips.

'Filling your time before Bianca arrives?' she
spiked. 'Just as you did in London.'

'Right first time,' he snapped back through bared
teeth. 'But this time you won't even get a phone call
when I've finished with you.'

'Your style of phone calls I can live without!' she
jerked back. 'The last was as cold and as impersonal
as you've turned out to be.'

'I don't pour my heart out to a bloody machine,'
he rasped. 'You weren't there——'

Gemma forced a cynical laugh. 'I'm beginning to
see it all now! I wasn't there, so the spurned hot-
blooded Latin boiled with misguided hurt. I have a
life, Felipe! I work for a living. Is that what got at
you, the fact that I'm an independent lady and I
wasn't sitting waiting breathlessly for your call? How
can you be so damned sexist when you were with
Bianca anyway?' Gemma cried back.

She wasn't going to take any more of this. It was
all so one-sided.

Felipe's eyes blazed like rampant bush fires. 'Our
worlds are poles apart but this could have been resolved if you'd given me the chance. You think you
are some sort of liberated lady, yet you act like a
Victorian maiden nursing her hurt pride. All you had
to do was pick up the phone, but you bloody well
didn't. That said one helluva a lot, sweet one. It
spelled out that all you cared about was what you

were getting every night and when it dried up you didn't want to know any more.'

'I don't want to be here,' she cried, turning away from him to collect up her brushes, her fingers tense and clumsy, her eyes smarting with unspent tears. 'I don't want any more of this, your filthy abuse, your tyrannical attitude. I don't want to paint Agustín's portrait. I just want to get back to England and forget your very existence.'

'It's not that easy, though, is it?'

'I'd say it's quite simple. My client isn't here. I can't waste any more of my valuable time waiting for him.'

'I mean it's not that simple for us. We can't forget each other's existence...' The change in his tone had her swinging round to face him.

Her heart tightened at the look in his eyes. For a second the fury had gone, and what took its place was far more terrifying.

She shook her head, trying to dispel the look that was frozen on her mind and had been all those months since they had loved each other so passionately. It was the look he gave her when he wanted her, wanted to make love to her. Words had never been needed; that languorous look had been enough. She had always gone to him and the feeling was still there. Even now, knowing how he meant to torment her, she still ached for him to take her in his arms. The old Felipe, though, she thought longingly, not this man who hurt her so.

'I want to leave,' she told him tightly, 'and I'd appreciate it if you made the arrangements for me.' Her eyes were wide and almost translucent with the depth of her appeal. He couldn't refuse her, surely?

A smile slicked across his face, slowly and dangerously.

'Dear, sweet Gemma. Did you think I would let you slip out of my life so easily again? I haven't finished with you yet. Apart from my wanting to torment the life from you in my bed, you have a job to do and if you walk out on the contract I'll let it be known that you're unreliable . . .'

'Don't threaten me, Felipe. Our worlds are different and you can't touch mine.'

'I believe Sir Ralph Pitton is your next commission and the one after that the Greek shipping magnate, Koztakis. Our worlds might be different, but in business it's a surprisingly small one. A word here, a word there . . .'

'You wouldn't!' Gemma breathed incredulously.

'I don't have to, Gemma,' was all he said. His hand came up and touched her chin, and the current that threaded through her body electrified her senses till they screamed. 'You'll stay because you want to,' he said so persuasively that she almost believed it all possible.

The touch on her chin deepened to a caress and Gemma lowered her black silky lashes to blot out the look in his eyes, that heavy-lidded sensual look that was so self-explanatory.

Need. It was there in his eyes and coursing through her body as their lips closed on each other's. Felipe's arms slid around her and six months of despair slid out of Gemma's heart. She clung to him desperately, willing a miracle, wishing it all could be right. But there was too much wrong knotted inside her and her emotions tangled obstructively. She couldn't breathe, she couldn't think when he held her like this, every touch urging her submission till she didn't know where or who she was.

Felipe's hands were skilful, smoothing over the old shirt she worked in, sliding it from her shoulders to reveal the straps of her sundress. His mouth grazed kisses over her naked flesh, burned into her skin, spurred the tears to her eyes.

A heartrending sob of despair tore from her throat, and, startled, Felipe drew back from her.

It was just the release she hadn't had the strength to engineer herself. She stepped back from him, hating herself for her weakness, hating him for his strength in pulling back from her. With trembling fingers she drew the old shirt back over her shoulders.

'Please let me go,' she pleaded without looking at him.

He lifted her chin and she was dismayed to see the hardness in his eyes once again.

'Let you go, just when it's getting interesting? No chance, Gemma. I shall keep you here till I've taken my fill of you, only then will I let you go, and by then you will be spoiled for ever more. You won't want another man after me, sweet one. I'm going to bed you so thoroughly you won't know what's hit you. London was just the foreplay.'

He turned from her then. Left her shivering by the sink with the intensity of his threats. She was afraid, so terribly afraid that every word he said was leaden with the cruel truth.

CHAPTER FOUR

GEMMA'S suitcase was half packed before he appeared in the doorway. She was going. She had decided. Nothing was going to stop her. Felipe stood watching her, leaning casually on the doorpost as if he had nothing better to do with his time.

'You're not going anywhere, Gemma,' he said at last, so predictably that she nearly laughed in his face. 'So take all that out of your case.'

'I'll do no such thing,' she told him tightly. 'And before you start making puerile excuses why I can't leave, I've already seen Mike in the gardens with Christina. I'll ask him to fly me out. That's if you don't mind; tough if you do!' she added sarcastically.

'I do mind, as it happens, but that doesn't matter because you've missed Mike.' He glanced at his watch. 'You'll hear the thrust of the engines shortly.'

Gemma saw triumph in his eyes and at the same time heard the jet roaring in the distance. Damn! If she'd been five minutes earlier she could have been with him. Furiously she balled a silk scarf in her fist and flung it into her case.

'Has he gone to pick up Agustín?' she asked, tight-lipped.

It made little difference to her intentions if he had. She was going, portrait or not. Apparently Agustín wanted this portrait as much as he craved a hole in the head, so both of them would be happy if she terminated the agreement. She wasn't even curious to meet him any more. She wanted out from Felipe's life and that was all.

'Agustín won't be back for a few days yet. Mike has gone to pick up supplies. You may have noticed that there isn't a supermarket in the immediate vicinity and——'

'Spare me the boring details of your domestic problems. When will Mike be back?'

'A couple of hours, by which time I will have persuaded you to stay.'

Gemma's eyes widened. 'This must sound like a remarkably stupid question in the circumstances, but however do you propose doing that?' she cut back sarcastically.

'Somehow I don't think sweeping you into my arms and softening you with sensual kisses would go down too well at the moment,' he drawled, changing his position to fold his arms across his chest and cross one leg over the other.

Gemma fumed. Was this the next phase of the torment game? Trying to humour her?

'Sensual kisses, diamonds, fast cars—nothing would persuade me to stay. I hope that satisfies you.'

'Only you in my bed tonight will give me any satisfaction.'

Her head jerked up at that and angrily she swept her hair from her face and tucked it behind her ears.

'You're in for a frustrating night, then, because you'll have to thrash it out on your own!'

'Now why should I have to do that when I have you here? Sorry, sweet one, but there is no way you are leaving and that is as certain as the sun rising in the morning.'

'So I'm a prisoner here?'

'Precisely, and prisoners do as they are told. So unpack that case before the warder loses his temper.'

She knew then that she hadn't a chance. But what was the answer? Simply to let him have his way and suffer? The question and the answer was beyond her capabilities of reasoning at the moment.

'Leave me alone, Felipe,' she uttered wearily. 'I'm bored with the game.'

'I'll have to think up some original moves, then. Can't have you stifling a yawn as I'm making love to you.' He eased himself away from the doorjamb. 'I'll see you at dinner.'

She heard his steps on the stone floor as he walked down the corridor, and then a door slamming shut. She thought he must be in the next room, though the walls were so old and thick that she heard no other sounds.

Crossly she shoved her suitcase off the bed and lay down, curling herself into a ball and biting her clenched fist. She might as well be in chains for the freedom she had. Prisoner and warder, it was a fact.

Reluctantly she dressed for dinner. She put on a black silk camisole top with matching baggy pants that whispered around her long legs, and her only jewellery was chunky gold swirl earrings. She made the effort because she knew it would infuriate him if she sulked another night in her room. She didn't want any more abuse. She wasn't weakening, she challenged herself, but there were ways of handling this, and antagonising him further wasn't one of them.

'I remember that perfume, Cassini, isn't it? "A love-affair that never ends",' he breathed seductively as he took her elbow at the head of the stairs.

She'd heard his door close after him as she was walking down the corridor but she hadn't stopped.

'Yes, it was a favourite of yours, wasn't it?' she murmured, unable to resist baiting him in spite of her resolutions not to.

'You know what that perfume does to me; it arouses me. Is that why you are wearing it?'

'To tease you, you mean?' she asked mock innocently as they walked down the stairs together.

'There's no point in trying to do that. I'm going to have you, tease or not. Maybe you feel the need to hot up the pace, though. Getting frustrated, are you?'

'Not for your body, Felipe,' she told him coldly.

'Not yet,' he whispered, increasing the pressure on her elbow with brute strength. 'But you'll be screaming for it soon enough.'

She held her breath in fury for a second, then. 'So will you, so let's see who screams first, shall we?'

He threw his head back and laughed and, though he hadn't had the last word, he roared as if he had.

He guided her through the sitting-room to the terrace, which reminded Gemma of the first time he had taken her elbow and guided her into his world of love and sensuality. Unwanted *frissons* of never-forgotten passions surged through her, flushing her cheeks in the mercifully dark night.

'Do you mind eating outside? I usually do when I'm here.'

'It's fine with me,' she told him stiffly. She wasn't going to be objectionable, at least not over where they ate.

One of the tables on the terrace had already been set for two so it would have made no difference if she had objected. There was a white linen damask cloth

with candles and flowers and crystal set on it. The
terrace was lit with concealed lighting that glowed
rather than glared. It was beautiful, heady and
dangerous.

The food was delicious, roast beef and an as-
sortment of vegetables. Gemma started well, bravely
ate, but found the rich red wine more tempting than
the food. The atmosphere between her and Felipe was
thick enough to slice.

She needed insensibility to get through the night,
but drink wasn't the answer. She refused a second glass
of wine and noticed Felipe didn't refill his own glass
either.

Maria tended to their needs and each time she came
to the table her presence eased the tension that hung
heavy in the night air. But once they were alone again
the conversation became spiked and cruel.

'So you have decided to stay. I didn't have to work
on you so very hard after all,' he iced after Maria had
cleared the plates from the table.

'I decided nothing. You passed the sentence and
I'm serving my time. I have no choice but to stay—
till my commission is completed, that is. And, talking
of my commission, I wonder what your employer
would think of this torment game of yours?' She
hoped a small threat might ease off the pressure.

'You keep referring to it as a game, Gemma. A
game it isn't. I take rejection seriously, and your punishment I am taking seriously too. As far as Agustín
is concerned, forget running to him with your troubles.
He has scant regard for women's feelings and not even
you could soften his heart. Besides, by the time he
returns it will all be over.'

'As quick as that,' Gemma retorted drily. 'Two, three days. You reckon you'll have me on my knees in that short time?'

'Well, I don't want to rush it,' he flinted back.

Gemma reached for the bottle of wine. She needed another drink after all. Felipe's hand closed over hers.

'No way, sweet one. I want you sober. I want you feeling every kiss, every caress, every last thrust.' His dark eyes glinted ferociously in the candlelight, as if he were some predatory creature of the forest.

Gemma's eyes flickered uncertainly but her heart steeled. 'I've already told you, Felipe. You will be wasting your time. You can't torment me. You can tempt me and you might succeed in possessing my body but that will be all. You can kiss and caress and thrust to your heart's content, but the most important part of me you'll never touch. I'll block off my emotions and my heart and I'll never give you the satisfaction of thinking you have hurt me.'

If she thought she had troubled him with that she was mistaken. He smiled without mirth.

'You forget, Gemma, I have loved you before. I know every part of you. What turns you on, what arouses you, what has you writhing and moaning for more. You can block off, sweet one, but one dark lonely night you'll wake up screaming for it and you'll be alone. No Felipe, and no other man will be able to do for you what I can. You know it and I know it and any amount of denial won't make the need go away.'

Gemma lowered her eyes and fought the truth of that brutal statement. Felipe was the essential lover, and when he had walked out on her she had known no other man could ever take his place. You couldn't top perfection, and she didn't even want to try. True it all might be, but Felipe had forgotten one thing.

She raised her eyes to meet his. 'And you, Felipe?' she started softly. 'You forget the passion I can so skilfully arouse in you. You yourself admitted that no other woman could ever turn you on the way I do. Or maybe all men say that, I wouldn't know. All I do know is that I've lived without your passion these last six months, whereas you seemed to have had a struggle.'

He smiled cynically. 'Which proves that my feelings for you were deeper than yours for me. That's a pity. It makes the task harder for me. I thought you might have some feelings left for me, but then love was a charade to you, wasn't it? Sex held us together for that week——'

'Stop it, Felipe,' Gemma pleaded in a husky whisper. How could he bring their affair down to gutter level like this? 'You know that wasn't true.'

'You cared for me, did you?' His voice was thick with sarcasm. 'Strange way you English have of showing it. You don't trust. A weakness you will pay for.'

They sat in silence as Maria returned with coffee and brandy. She poured the coffees for them, her black eyes flicking uncertainly between the two of them. Did she sense the atmosphere? She must; it was heavy enough.

Gemma wondered what Felipe was thinking— maybe the same train of thought she was taking. Going back over all they had been to each other in London and asking why it had soured so badly. Mistrust, misunderstanding, or was it simply that their love was just not meant to be? If only she had made that phone call, swallowed her hurt and her pride and given him a chance to redeem himself—but would it have made it all right? How could it have done? He had gone away with Bianca and, though she had never known that for sure, she had convinced herself it was so. But suppose...

'You did go to New York with Bianca, didn't you?' She held her heart on freeze, waiting for his reply. Though what difference if he hadn't? He had already admitted his cousin was a part of his life, more than her.

'We had a very interesting week together, yes. Almost as *stimulating* as our week together,' he told her, laying cruel emphasis on the word stimulating.

How easily he could torment her. He didn't have to threaten to take her to bed to do it. The thought of him and Bianca together was enough to have her heart screaming in agony.

'And yet you persist in trying to hurt me for some triviality. I was the injured party, Felipe. You seem determined not to acknowledge that.'

'Do you expect me to?' His smile was thin and contemptuous. 'How little you know of the South American man.'

'Funny how your nationality suddenly seems to be an excuse for your disgusting behaviour.' Gemma drained her brandy. 'And for your promiscuity,' she added as she lowered her empty glass to the table.

'And what is your excuse? I thought the English were so frigid.'

'Not at all, just choosy. And all I can offer for an excuse for my own wanton behaviour is that I took you on face value, not what was stamped on your passport.'

He smiled cynically. 'Ah, if only we had known the depths of our differences then.'

'If only,' Gemma uttered sarcastically. 'If only you had presumed my frigidity and I had presumed your licentiousness——'

'What a lot we would have missed.'

She wanted to smile at that, but she didn't. 'But we would have avoided all this, though,' she told him mournfully, immediately wishing she had held her tongue. It was almost an admission that he was getting to her.

He was on to it as rapidly as a whippet to a lame rabbit. 'So my revenge is affecting you at last?'

'Not the effect you wish for, though. I'd rather live without your gibes, yes, but I'll put up with them.'

'And you'll suffer my lovemaking with a traditional stiff upper lip, will you?'

'If it gets that far I'll lie back and think of England, yes.'

He laughed and shook his head. 'How sweetly you try to evade the truth.'

'Oh, and what is that truth?'

'That your mother country will be the last thought in your mind when I make love to you.'

'My patriotism means more to me than your groping!' she flung back at him, pretty feebly, she thought as soon as it was out.

'We'll see about that.'

'Yes, we will!' she retorted. 'And now I want to go to bed.' She stood up and flung her crumpled napkin down on the table.

'You always were a fast worker.'

'I didn't mean that,' she rasped impatiently. 'I meant——'

'I know what you meant,' he interjected, and rose to his feet. For a blissful second she thought he was going to let her go, but how naïve could you get? His hand snaked out across the table, grasping her wrist before she had the wit to snatch it away. He pulled her round the table to him, crushed her in his arms. She steeled her lips for his penetration but it was useless. He took her fully, expertly, parting her lips so skilfully that he might have had a degree in kissing.

How tempted she was to let him take it all. Her body, her heart, her love. Then perhaps he would leave her in peace. She would end up a shadow of her former self, but wasn't she already a shadow of the confident woman she had once been? She had run the gamut of emotions these last months; to run through them again wouldn't be such a hardship. But it would, it would, her heart screamed as his hands caressed over her breasts, the fine silk of her camisole top seeming to heighten the hedonism he had threatened.

She hated him now, despised him, and yet every stroke he smoothed over her aching nipples was a condemnation of that hatred. How could you hate and love and want? How could your body lead you away from all that your sensibilities rallied against?

His hand slid under the silk to her naked flesh, burning her skin till the pain was almost intolerable. The torture of need; it hurt so badly that she wanted to forget his cruelty and give in to its pull. She wanted to melt under his strokes, to murmur that she adored and wanted him more than ever, but it was precisely what he wanted to hear, so that he could punish her with some cruel rejection. She wouldn't be able to live with that.

Tears scoured her eyes. She was close, though, verging dangerously near to giving in. Pulses throbbed urgently within her as his kisses deepened to the intensity where soon there would be no going back.

'No!' she cried, tearing her mouth from his.

His hold on her tightened. 'Painful, is it?' he growled in her ear, his hand coming up to grip the weight of her hair at the nape of her neck. 'You're not alone, *querida*.' He pulled her hard into him, urging himself against her so she could feel the effect she had on him. 'You can feel my pain too, can't you? It's tangible. I can't come out of this unscathed, I assure you.'

'Why, then?' she murmured helplessly. 'Why put yourself through this as well?'

'So you admit it, that I'm hurting you?' He grazed the words across her throat.

'You know you are,' she finally admitted, closing her eyes against the onslaught of his lips on her heated flesh. 'But why pain yourself? Just let me go, Felipe. Don't do this.'

'Don't do this,' he echoed derisively, snaking his tongue over the soft hollow of her throat. 'Don't you understand what fires me? I want to exorcise you out of my life.' He cupped her face in his hands and looked at her then. 'I hate loving you, do you know that? I hate the nights when I can't sleep for the need to possess you. I hate myself for allowing you that power over me——'

It was then she tore herself away from him, somehow finding the strength to put air and space between them. She stood there, trembling from head to toe. 'And you're going to punish me for something within yourself you can't control. I feel sorry for you...' she breathed.

He smiled coldly. 'Don't waste sympathy on me, Gemma. Save it for yourself, because whatever I suffer you'll pay doubly for. Now go to bed and see how far into the night you can get without thinking of my mouth on yours, my caresses...'

She turned and ran then with a sob trapped dangerously in her throat, threatening to choke the life from her. She wanted to die rather than stay another night in this place, she realised as she reached her room, her breath coming in deep rasps, her lungs burning with exertion.

She lurched to the window, furiously swept aside the lace and breathed the night-scented air. It was cloying and humid and she clutched at her throat, horrified to realise that she was crying. Oh, Felipe, she mouthed into the still air.

She awoke in the small hours of the morning and didn't know why. It was seconds before it hit her. She was feverishly hot and she'd been having a bad dream. Felipe had been loving her, as he had in London. Not cruelly and punishingly but with tenderness and care, his lips and his sensuous touch powering her to the brink of that sweet ecstasy that hovered on the edge of reality. But in real life Felipe had fulfilled every secret promise during their lovemaking. The dream was murderously different, Felipe scorning her just as she was about to lose control, a wicked smile on his mouth as he brought her nearer and nearer to the edge of her orgasm, and then drawing back from her with a leonine roar of triumph...

Gemma sat up in the heated darkness, covered her face with her hands. It had started, the torment he

had promised. Not a night had passed since Felipe
had left her without her thinking of him, imagining
him back in her life and loving her as if Bianca had
never existed. And now he *was* back in her life and
it was all so cruelly different. Her love and need were
still there but Felipe's had distorted to bitter revenge.
And he was winning, she knew that. The ache inside
her confirmed it. She wanted him and would always
want him and it was a wicked sentence to have to live
with.

Gemma heard the row as soon as she hit the bottom
of the stairs the next morning.

She stood still, trying to gauge where it was coming
from. Agustín's study, but there was only one voice—
Felipe's.

'I've had enough, Agustín! Get rid of her... I'm
not going to do it... Like hell I will!'

Gemma was in time to see Felipe slam down the
telephone receiver and lean heavily on the desk, his
fists bunched tightly. He had his back to her as she
stood in the open doorway and his head was lowered.

Cold fear ran through her at what she had heard,
the content and the bitterness of the deliverance.
Suddenly he wanted rid of her and was expecting
Agustín to do it for him. She hurried away to the
kitchen before he turned and caught her
eavesdropping.

'I have no work today,' Christina told Gemma as
she served up her breakfast. 'I sit all day for you.'

She was very eager to see herself immortalised on
canvas and Gemma forced a smile. She was still in
shock after hearing that snippet of conversation on
the phone. 'That's fine with me, but——'

'But not fine with me,' Felipe interrupted, coming into the kitchen like a thunderbolt.

Christina flushed hotly and Gemma steeled herself. Whatever Agustín's reply, it hadn't been balm to his ears. Felipe was in a raging temper.

'You can have an hour of Gemma's time and that's all!' he directed firmly at Christina.

Christina nodded, quickly placed Felipe's breakfast on the table and hurried out of the room.

Desolately Gemma sat across from Felipe at the breakfast table and tried to eat.

'What's wrong with you?' he asked flintily.

'You,' she told him flatly. 'Bad temper puts me off my food.'

'What have you got to be bad-tempered about? Have a rough night, did you?' He poured her coffee for her and sugared it, just as he had in London. The gesture stung her.

'I'm not the one in a foul temper, you are! I had a splendid night's sleep if you must know,' she lied. 'You obviously didn't!'

'I'm not in a bad temper——'

'Well, I'd hate to be around you when you are!' she cut in.

'Give it time and you might see the full-blown strength of my wrath; in fact go on picking at your food and you might witness it sooner than you think. You know I can't stand messing with food.'

Gemma purposely twirled a slice of bacon round her plate, eventually abandoning it to toy with a piece of tomato.

'Don't be so bloody childish!' he ordered darkly.

'That's good coming from the past master of adult infancy——'

His hand clamped over hers to silence her, nearly crushing the fine bones of her fingers in his.

'That hurts,' she murmured.

'Good, it was meant to.' He let her go and she rubbed her fingers, exaggeratedly because she didn't want him to know that he hadn't hurt her that much.

'Why do you suddenly want rid of me?' she asked boldly.

He frowned. 'What are you talking about?'

Nothing for it but to be honest. 'I overheard your phone call with Agustín.'

'Checking up on me again——'

'No!' Gemma snapped. 'I don't creep around trying to keep tabs on you, I'm not interested enough. But you were bellowing at the top of your voice and no doubt the whole household heard.'

'So what did you hear?'

'That you wanted rid of me and for Agustín to do it.'

'Heard your name mentioned, did you?' he came back, sarcastically.

Gemma bit her lip. 'No... no, I just presumed...'

'You presumed wrong, then. In future don't listen to calls that have nothing to do with you.'

She wondered who he had been talking about, in that case. Maybe one of the staff? She didn't ask.

'I want to use the studio before Agustín gets back,' she told him, picking up her knife and fork and continuing with her breakfast.

'No problem.'

Surprised, she glanced up at him. She had expected an objection. He glanced at his watch and she realised he wasn't being suddenly soft with her; he simply didn't have the time to argue.

'I thought I would use Christina as a dry run for Agustín . . .'

'Do as you please,' he murmured, dabbing at his mouth with his napkin. He stood up.

'Where are you going?' It was out before she could stop it, the stupid question that had him raising his brow mockingly.

'You sound just like an English wife,' he said, surprisingly softly, and bent and cupped her chin, held her head steady to kiss her full on the mouth. 'Be here when I get back,' he ordered after taking his fill.

'And you sound like a bastard Latin husband,' she murmured under her breath as he strode out of the back door, slapping his crop against his riding boots as he went out.

After she had finished her coffee she went in search of Christina. An hour, Felipe had said, but he hadn't stated which hour. Perhaps it would be better to get it over and done with while he was out riding.

She checked the studio before finding Christina. It was spotless. Someone had been ordered to clean it up. Obviously not Christina, who stood hesitantly at the studio door, as nervous as a cat urged to jump in a whirling river.

'Is all right?' she asked Gemma, her dark eyes wide. 'Only I never see before. Señor de Navas he no like anyone here.'

The thought made Gemma nervous as she pushed open the door for Christina as if they were opening up the tomb of Tutankhamun. Christina made Agustín sound like an ogre, Felipe was at war with him, and the man concerned was her father! She wondered how Felipe would feel if he knew. She locked away the conjectures as her mother had locked away her secret so many years ago. For the first time she could see her mother's point in trying to stop her coming.

The hour passed quickly, with Christina relaxing and telling Gemma all about her romance with Mike; how Mike intended to join a major airline company in North America and take Christina with him. They would travel the world together and Gemma realised with a jolt that the girl had only ever been as far as Caracas in her life. She envied her simplicity and contentment and she envied her her love.

'I worry about Señor de Navas, he no like, but Felipe he say OK, so OK it must be,' Maria muttered when she brought them a cold drink as they were finishing the session.

'You mean opening up the studio?'

'*Si*. He never open this studio after the day he marry.'

'It was here before he married?' Gemma quizzed, knowing she shouldn't probe but finding it irresistible.

'*Si*. Señor de Navas he go to Europe for a long time, business for his father. He meet an artist lady, like you,' Maria laughed. 'The studio he made for her but she no come. Then he marry——' She stopped suddenly, looking over Gemma's shoulder to the door and the walkway and the double doors of Agustín's study.

They were wide open and Gemma suspected that by the look of astonishment on Maria's and Christina's faces that this was the first time. Felipe was coming towards them.

'We go,' Maria murmured, giving her daughter a look.

Gemma was cleaning her brushes at the sink when he strode into the studio.

'Do you always have that effect on Agustín's staff, send them scuttling...?'

'I scuttle no one,' he told her.

'They left in a hurry.'

'They have duties. Maria is an excellent house-keeper and her schedule is rigid. It's good,' he said, and Gemma whirled from the sink to see what had changed his conversation. He was studying the picture of Christina.

Gemma tried to stem the flood of colour that rushed to her face at the sight of him standing before the canvas. Her heart tightened painfully. He was still wearing his riding gear, calf-hugging white jodhpurs that were now dusty and scuffed. His black polo shirt was taut with moisture across his chest and his hair and brow were wet as if he'd just put his head under the water pump after a vigorous ride. She could smell the maleness of him, the mixture of his cologne and his own personal muskiness. The brushes slid from her grasp into the sink.

She concentrated on gathering them up and washing them briskly, fighting with horror her treacherous arousal at the sight and smell of such raw maleness.

'You forget, I know you, Gemma,' he murmured in her ear, sliding his arms around her waist and pressing himself hard into her back.

'Don't do that!' she cried, twisting to get out of his grasp. He tightened his grip on her and his arms locked painfully round her till she could hardly draw breath.

'I always aroused you after working out, didn't I? But I haven't been working out this morning, sweet one. I've been urging my stud horse on——'

'Stop it!' she husked, struggling hard within the re-striction of his arms. Suddenly she was spun around

to face him and his grip tightened painfully on her
upper arms and he was pressing against her so hard
the edge of the sink bit into her back.

'You should have come and watched, *querida*; it
only takes a few thrusts and it's all over——'

'That sort of thing turns you on, does it? You're
an animal yourself!' she gasped.

'No, you are. A very sexy animal, and *you* turn me
on, not my horses.' His mouth was tantalising on hers,
tempting her yet holding back his passion till he was
sure she was going with him.

Desperately Gemma fought him, with her physical
strength, which was feeble against his, her fists making
no contact with his chest as he caught her wrists and
forced them to her side. But he could do little with
her inner fight. That was all down to her and treach-
erously she could feel it sliding recklessly away from
her. And he knew just when the slide was out of her
control, storming downhill, gathering momentum as
it went. Then his kisses heightened to that level of
passion when to join him was inevitable.

Together, locked together, her reserve was gone. He
knew exactly the moment to release her wrists to let
them come up and graze helplessly through his damp
hair. A groan as deep as an ocean came to his lips
and she felt it reverberate against her breast as he tore
her shirt open.

Suckling her nipples like a hungry child, he forced
her down on to the divan. The contact of the warm
silk on her back had her crying a feverish 'No!' but
it was useless; any protestation was lost on a gushing
wave of desire as he lowered himself down beside her.

His mouth on hers was relentless as his hands
powered over her body, skilfully manipulating her out

of her old painting shirt. Apart from tiny silk bikini briefs she was naked beneath it.

His dark, hooded eyes raked her near naked form before he lowered his mouth to her stomach, running his tongue across her pulsing flesh till she was gasping with frustration.

This was the torment she had dreamed about last night, when he had held back from her, leaving her suspended and aching for the release he was tempting her with now. But dreams were misleading and she realised that Felipe wasn't stopping, not yet anyway.

Her briefs were eased aside and his thumb grazed sensuously across her triangle of dark silken hair, his rhythmic pressure, searching and finding. And then gently, oh, so gently his caress deepened and the pulsing rhythm spun her nearer and nearer to the edge of ecstasy. She knew, in that exquisite, reckless moment of near abandon, she knew that he wasn't going to stop at all. How clever he was, how well he knew her. His revenge would be more subtle than the tease of her nightmare.

Her mouth opened in a sob of anguish. 'Please, Felipe . . .'

Her voice echoed and so did his soft moan of triumph as his strokes quickened, unrestricted and confident because he knew she was beyond the realms of reality. Gemma came in a rush of fury and white heat that had her struggling helplessly against the inevitable. His mouth over hers stemmed the core of her anguished cry for the pain and the torment of his bitter revenge.

His breath was deep against her throat and in the midst of her own torture she knew he was hurting too. She couldn't stop the tears then. They flowed for herself and for him and for their love that had gone terribly wrong.

Felipe mouthed the wet from her cheeks and then he eased away to look down on her and to run a hand through her thick luxuriant mane. He opened his mouth to speak and Gemma tensed fiercely in preparation for the cruel gibe she sensed was coming.

His fingers caressed her hair, twisting the tendrils possessively round his fingers. 'It suits you longer,' he murmured softly. 'If you hadn't been so untrusting, Gemma, I would have been around to see this grow.' And then his eyes glazed with anger as if he'd been cheated and he thrust the tendrils across her face, stood up from the couch and walked away from her without looking back.

CHAPTER FIVE

IT WAS worse than Gemma could ever have anticipated. Felipe's cruelty and total humiliation had
rocked her. She had avoided him for two days now.
Or maybe it had been the other way round, he had
avoided her. She was too stunned to fathom it out.
All she knew was she had seen nothing of him and
somehow that was worse than a head-on
confrontation.

He had known precisely what he had done to her.
The humiliation had been the lesser of the two evils
to suffer. He knew that that sort of one-sided lovemaking only made her crave him more.

Gemma despised herself and hated Felipe for
making her feel that way. She still loved and wanted
a man who was hard and cruel and had no regard to
the pain he was inflicting on her. But those wonderful
days in London couldn't be erased from her mind and
that was the trouble, the problem she was fighting to
understand. They had been in love then, and Felipe
had been the ultimate lover. How could he have
changed so? If he really did still love her, how could
he hurt her and keep on hurting her? How could he
himself hold back from taking her when once their
lovemaking had been so vital and complete?

'Agustín will be back tomorrow night.'

Gemma whirled from the final touches she had been
making to Christina's picture. It would be dark soon

and she was nearly finished. It had filled her time and she was grateful to have been absorbed.

'Good,' she murmured, turning back to the canvas, not wanting to look at him. He appeared no different and she knew she did. She had noticed the blueness under her eyes this very morning and her eyes had lost the last vestige of brightness they had been hanging on to these past months. She looked and felt dull and heavy.

'Are you pleased with it?' he asked, standing just behind her.

'Yes,' she answered not offering more. 'What time will he be here?'

'For dinner at nine. You will dress, of course. So tonight will be our last night together. You will undress, of course.'

Gemma swung round furiously. 'I don't even find that remotely amusing!' she blazed.

'I don't suppose you do.' His mouth twisted into a mockery of a smile. 'Fact is, it wasn't meant to be funny. I take my sex seriously.'

'Well, you can take your serious sex somewhere else. If you must know, and no doubt this will give you enormous pleasure, you have won, Felipe. You have hurt me, tortured me, humiliated me and there is nothing more to be done.' Her eyes were cold as ice as she gazed up at him.

'Nothing more to be done, eh? You might not think so but I beg to differ. I want complete satisfaction, sweet one, sexually and mentally. I want you sobbing in my arms, too exhausted to speak. I want you leaving here a broken woman.'

'And I want you dead!'

He smiled and tilted her chin with the tip of his finger. 'A dead lover is no good to you at all.'

'A live one isn't exactly doing my health a lot of good either!'

'*Si, querida*, I see that in your eyes. Could it be that you are not sleeping well? Could it be that you long for my touch?'

'Could it be that you make me sick—physically?'

His mouth closed over hers and as always she was badly prepared. Would she ever get her timing right? She had imagined this, reacted violently to his imagined touch. In dreamland she could cope but in life it was all so hopeless.

His hand stroked the pale column of her throat and she tried to arch away from him but he stilled her with one powerful hand at the small of her back.

The kiss deepened, passionately, and real fear gripped at Gemma's stomach. He wanted her and this was no tease. But no, not now, not ever.

She tore her mouth from his and pushed at his shirtfront with her clenched fists. His hands clasped her wrists tightly to him and then he forced her hands down.

'You bastard!' she breathed, squeezing her eyes tightly shut.

'Touch me,' he husked, stilling her balled fists with the caress of his thumbs.

'Never!'

'Do it, Gemma.' His tone had changed dramatically. It had softened and husked and instantly it aroused her.

Appalled at herself, she tried to prevent her fists uncoiling, but it was impossible. They had a will of their own, were as detached from her body as her reasoning was. His denim jeans were rough to the touch and her fingers trembled. Slowly she opened her eyes to look at him as her fingers stroked and smoothed over him. His eyes darkened till they were black and his lids were heavy and hooded with desire.

She knew she should pull away, ease up the pressure and show him she was capable of inflicting pain too. But he moved against her hand and she was mesmerised and knew she couldn't torture him. It wasn't in her and yet she had suffered and he would make her suffer more but still she was incapable of hurting him.

He released her hands when he was sure she wouldn't lash out at him and he cupped her face and kissed her lips, still keeping up a gentle rhythmic pulse against her groin.

When he kissed her like this she was filled with hope that he wouldn't go through this punishing agony any longer, that suddenly he would whisper to her that he loved her and wanted her and that revenge was anything but sweet.

His hands came behind her to grip her hips and he stilled himself against her. 'Later, *querida*, later,' he murmured throatily.

'Again!' she sobbed in a hushed whisper, her eyes wide with horror. 'Is there no end to your damned cruelty? Stop it, Felipe, I beg you to stop it!'

He held her twisting body still but now she was strong with fury and she twisted viciously from him. She said nothing but on a sob tore from the studio.

She flung herself on the bed in her room and gazed up at the fan whirring overhead. The throb of the rattan blades matched the throb of anxiety in her head and the dull throbbing ache of her need.

He had done it again, tempted her, seduced her till she couldn't recognise right from wrong. But what, in God's name, was he doing to himself? She couldn't begin to understand the depth of his thinking. They were different of course, not just by gender, but by their birth. She was European, he a fiery Latin American. South America wasn't another planet, she had told her mother, but it was. An entirely different constellation.

Later she stood by the window, gazing out at the heavenly bodies, and a thought, so strange, suddenly hit her. She was Agustín de Navas's daughter. She was partly South American herself! She was rolling this thought around in her mind when she heard a movement at the door.

'You refuse to eat with me.'

He was standing in the doorway in his evening suit and her heart tugged furiously. She had fallen in love with him in his evening suit. His elegance and his power in black never ceased to impress her. She turned back to gaze at the stars, determined to fight the weakness within her. 'What did you expect?' she said baldly.

'I expected you to dine with me . . .'

'And then you expected to come up here and make love to me?'

'Why not? It's what we both want, isn't it?'

She heard his step coming closer behind her and her hands tightened on the stone windowsill. She wished she were dressed. After telling Maria she didn't want dinner that night she had bathed and got ready for bed. She wore nothing under her satin robe, nothing but regret for her stupidity and shortsightedness. He would make something of it, she felt sure.

'You're even prepared for me,' he murmured, and turned her to face him.

'I should know you by now, shouldn't I? You see my robe as your come-on. I had an early night in mind, Felipe; not with you, though.'

'And you didn't have anyone else in mind, did you?' he said knowingly.

'How conceited you are,' she breathed. 'Do you really believe I've had no one since you?' Perhaps this was the answer; it was self-deprecating, but it was worth making herself cheap to be free of his demands.

'For all I know you could have bedded your way through the entire mounted Household Cavalry, but one thing I believe—none of them can give you what I can.'

'Satisfaction?' she sneered up at him. 'Your life appears to revolve around sex, Felipe. You talk of torment and revenge and it is all sexually orientated. What about feelings, caring, sharing, having fun together? And I don't mean the romping-around-in-bed sort of fun!'

'Love and sex are equal partners in my life, Gemma. I can't do one without the other any more. It's why, since you, I can't make it with another woman——'

'You've tried, have you?' she bit out. What a stupid question! He had Bianca, hadn't he?

He didn't answer that childish retort but went on, 'It's why you will pay for your enslavement. You have ruined my life . . .'

She pushed past him and went to the door and held it open for him.

'You ruined your own life by walking out on me and going away with your cousin. You can walk out of this room now, Felipe, because I'm not taking any more blame for your mental state.'

'But you'll take full responsibility for my physical state,' he told her brutally.

She didn't know how he had done that, manifested himself across the room with the speed of light. His hand came up over her head and she flinched, thinking he was going to strike her. His force went to the door, slamming it shut behind her. She was pressed against it, his hands each side of her on the panelling, imprisoning her, before she had time to draw another breath.

'What ... what are you going to do?' she husked nervously.

'What are *we* going to do, *querida*? Do you want us to talk through it all first? I remember you used to like that. Our love talk. What I was going to do to you and what you were going to——'

She ducked and tried to get out from him but again he was quicker. He caught her and spun her into his arms.

'Where the hell do you think you are running to? The bed maybe? Can't you wait for the preliminaries, sweet one? You always were so damned tantalisingly eager.'

Her hand came up then. Her small, artistic palm with the sudden strength of ten men, meant to strike him hard across the side of his face, but it never made contact. He grasped it, his reactions astonishingly quick. His eyes locked with hers and there was no war in their lustrousness but something she hadn't seen

for a long time. Slowly he raised her palm to his
mouth.

Her breath caught in her throat at the tenderness
of his kiss and the silkiness of his tongue as he ran it
over the soft flesh, which seared and stung as if it had
actually made contact with his face. Her head went
back against the door and she closed her eyes tightly,
desperately trying to hold back the tears. She had seen
love in his eyes and had felt it in the tenderness of his
lips, and this couldn't be more torment, surely?

Oh, God. It was going to happen and she had no
control. The fight was gone, her longing filling every
part of her, leaving no room for fear.

'Felipe, please don't,' she murmured weakly, and
then there were no more words. Tenderly his lips
moved to her wrists, gauging her pulse with the tip
of his tongue, and as if her racing pulse-rate was what
he was seeking to give him reason to go on he swept
her into his arms and carried her to the bed.

The soft candle-lights on the walls cast golden light
over him as he started the disrobing ritual that had
been the prelude to their love-affair. Gemma lay on
the bed watching him, her heart crying within her
breast. He was going to make love to her and whatever
followed didn't matter. She loved him, wanted him,
and, if this was the last time, so be it.

He stood naked by the bed looking down at her.
There was no cruelty in his eyes to torment her with,
no knowing smirk of bitterness on his face, just the
need that echoed hers.

Slowly she sat up, her silken robe parting to reveal
the eager swell of her breasts. Felipe let out a moan
of anticipation as she edged towards him. Her lips
smoothed over his silken arousal and he let out

another moan, one of complete surrender this time. His hands tenderly gripped the side of her head and he splayed his fingers in her hair. Gemma closed her mouth around him, rejoicing in the tremor that ran through him as her tongue and the sweet inner warmth of her lips encompassed his arousal.

'Dear God, how I've missed you,' he grated, a throaty admission that filled Gemma's heart with joy.

She drew back from him then and looked up, her eyes wide and misty with the love he must be able to read. He bent to kiss her mouth, to taste himself on her lips, and then he came down to lie with her, his kisses taking on the power she had so longed for, the power of his love and his sexuality. Love and sex, he'd said—for him they were equal so this could not be a punishment, it just couldn't.

His hands moved over every inch of her heated flesh, rediscovering her flawless skin, arousing what she had longed for every barren night of her life since he had left her. He kissed every part of her from the scented hollow of her throat to the silken plains of her stomach, from the swollen peaks of her breasts to the soft triangle of dark hair between her long graceful thighs.

Felipe drew back from her and watched her face as his fingers moved languidly over her inner thighs, tracing sensitive trails of expectation on her skin till she burned with need. She couldn't stop herself moving against his hand and then she tensed, so severely that he instantly eased off the pressure.

His voice came gravelled with remorse. 'No, this is no punishment . . .'

She twisted away from him, her eyes wide with fear and despair, her bottom lip trembling . . .

'No, *querida*,' he breathed urgently, 'it's not what you think.'

'How do I know that?' she sobbed, grasping at her robe. 'I told you you've won, isn't that enough for you?'

'No, it isn't enough!' he roared, his anger aroused so swiftly that a cry of fear caught in Gemma's throat. He grasped at her as she tried to slide from the bed, took her by the arms and threw her back on the lace cover. 'There is no going back, sweet one. And forget any ideas of holding back to torment *me*!' he panted. 'I'm going to have you——'

'You're going to have to force me!' she screamed, her heart racing so furiously that she thought it would burst.

He thrust his knee between her legs and her next cry was twisted and anguished and then something else that shocked her. She heard her own deep moan of submission and she could do nothing about it. To fight was useless; to admit that this was what she wanted was inevitable. Her fingers bit into the muscular flesh of his back and her hips arched forward wantonly.

He was inside her. With one swift persistent thrust he was inside her and she was holding him there, almost a reflex action as if that was her destiny in life.

'So this is force, is it, *querida*?' His voice was soft and mocking with leaden overtones of his sexual need. 'You were ready for me, welcoming me, and now you encompass me with your liquid love. I don't call that force, sweet one.'

He moved slowly, deliberate deep thrusts that had her husking his name and him breathing hers raggedly. Involuntarily her hands came up and raked frantically through his hair. She tried desperately not to think, to block off her emotions as she had vowed to him she would. But vows like that were null and void in actuality. She should have known, she should have prepared herself for the overpowering depth of his lovemaking and her rapacious need for it.

His muscular power inside her was no assurance of his love and yet... how could it not be when hers screamed out from every nerve-ending of her body?

Locked in a fury of urgent movement, they hurled out of control, their bodies thrusting and burning for release from the urgency and the heat, both desperate for the final triumph that would somehow ease both their agony.

She felt the give-away swell inside her and she went with him, not holding back but riding the crest of the life force that pumped urgently within her. He knew her well; knowing the depth and the extent of her orgasm, he stayed with her, beyond his own, kissing her feverishly to prolong the release, to enhance her joy.

When finally he collapsed beside her, reaching out to fold her into his arms, she knew his love for her was still there—buried under the deadly avalanche of his hurt pride, but nevertheless there. Hers pulsed within her as it always had, but there was no satisfaction in those thoughts.

She lay next to him, listening to his breathing, more even and regular now as he slid unerringly into sleep. What would happen now? Would he use her submission as a weapon to hurt her again and again? She buried her face in her pillow and didn't know. She loved a man she didn't know.

*   *   *

She awoke the next morning to find she was alone.
She rolled on to her stomach and clawed his pillow
towards her and clutched it fiercely. She could smell
him, his hair, his musky love scent. He had woken
her with sensual kisses in the darkness of the night,
sensual kisses that had quickly become a white-hot
fever as she had turned to him and given him every
part of her body and soul, and then later, much later,
they had slipped into an exhausted, love-sated sleep—
and now he was gone.

Gemma got up, flinging the pillow away from her.
She brutally showered away their love. She dressed
and went down to breakfast, took it alone in the airy
kitchen with Maria and Christina quietly discussing
the menu they were putting on for Agustín's return
that night.

Gemma swallowed her coffee hot and black. Her
father; she would come face to face with him tonight.
Where was the curiosity, the eagerness to meet him?
It was fluttering unwillingly in her breast like some
poor trapped butterfly. What beat fiercely inside her,
overbearing all else, was the thought of Felipe, who
had crept away from her bed, and her life, for all she
knew. She wasn't going to ask Maria where he was.
She didn't want to know, she really didn't.

That night as Gemma dressed for dinner she wondered where Felipe had been all day. She had swum
and sunbathed to pass the time but he hadn't made
an appearance. In one way the thought cheered her;
if he had meant revenge last night surely he would
have wanted to hammer it home—what better time
than the morning after the night before? But on the
other hand he might be feeling somewhat re-
pentant ... and pigs might fly.

She took a great deal of time over her appearance, not because it was necessary but she found it therapeutic. She dressed in a cool blue silk designer affair which added a satiny lustre to her golden skin, and as she flicked at her hair she heard the jet overhead and the butterfly trapped inside her found new life.

Nervously she waited in her room, waited to hear the car approaching from the airstrip. This was the moment she needed Felipe, but why, she wasn't sure. Moral support, perhaps. She had never felt more desperately lonely in her life.

She stood by the window to compose herself. It was like being poised on the end of a diving-board, plucking up the nerve to go in head first. It was then she heard laughter from the gardens below, recognised it though she had only heard it once before. In London, in a restaurant, the three of them.

Bianca was here at the Villa Verde! Her father and Bianca at one time? She couldn't take it! She couldn't!

Through her confusion she heard a door slam, Felipe's door. She launched herself out into the corridor.

'How could you!' she cried furiously. Now she knew the depth of his revenge. 'This is the ultimate torment, is it? Throw Bianca in my face after last night——'

He caught hold of her as she lunged for him, wanting to hurt him so badly that her strength was equal to a rogue elephant's. Felipe pinned her flaying arms to her side.

'Stop it, Gemma! For God's sake, stop it! I didn't know she was coming tonight. Agustín must have picked her up in Caracas and brought her here ahead of schedule.'

The strength zapped out of Gemma and she stared
stupidly up at him. Agustín had brought her from
Caracas? He must know her very well. Of course he
would, her fury told her. She was very much a part
of Felipe's life, and Felipe lived here and worked
here...

'Now calm down,' he told her firmly, his dark eyes
subduing her. 'I didn't plan this. It wasn't my intention to hurt you this way.'

'What difference?' she spat back at him. 'What
difference how you hurt me just so long as you do?
I'm not going down there...' She couldn't, not now
Bianca was here. If only Felipe knew what he had
done. Wasn't it enough she had to face her father for
the first time? Now this!

'Don't be so absurd, and remember why you are
here——'

'To do a job, yes, of course—during all the fun I
forget!' she snapped sarcastically.

'Cool it, Gemma.'

She fought the knotting of her stomach as he pro-
pelled her downstairs. Useless to argue, because in
her anguished state she might admit something she
didn't want to. 'Agustín de Navas is my father,' she
might scream at Felipe, 'and Bianca is your cousin
and mistress and aren't we all going to have a wonderful fun-packed night?'

They walked towards the drawing-room door where
drinks were to be served before dinner in the dining
hall. Was it her imagination, but was there even more
gloom settling over the house? The candle-lights
glowed brightly in the big hallway but the gloom was
atmospheric, with bad vibes that were almost tan-

gible. Maria was waiting to serve the drinks by the sideboard.

Agustín Delgado de Navas stood by the open doors leading to the terrace, his back to anyone who walked into the room. He didn't move when they entered the room though he couldn't have failed to know they were there; Gemma's heels had made enough noise on the terracotta tiles.

Though Gemma stood still she felt that every muscle was twitching as if in a final death throe. She didn't want to be here, seeing her father's back to her. He would turn, he had to turn, and then what?

Felipe moved across to Maria and helped her pour drinks then Maria left the room with a small smile for Gemma and it was just the three of them.

He turned at last, tall, almost as powerfully built as Felipe. His white dinner-jacket was superbly cut, leaving no doubt in anyone's mind that this was a wealthy man. Though he could be clad in worn denim, Gemma thought quickly, and the effect would have been the same. He simply looked highly successful.

Gemma had imagined this moment over and over again, had rehearsed her first words, anticipated his, but nothing had prepared her for the impact of coming face to face with the man who was her father.

She knew then how easily her mother must have fallen for the thirty-year-old Agustín de Navas. At fifty-seven he was devastating. Thick dark hair, silver at the temples. Dark eyes that penetrated hers like arrows of steel. His features were dramatically good-looking but his flesh deeply lined and tanned to a leathery hardness. His physique was superb, almost military in its bearing. He was a proud man, a striking man, a cold, hard man.

Felipe made the introductions, which Gemma only dimly heard. All she was aware of was this man standing in front of her, this man who was her father.

He scrutinised her for a full minute, which felt like an hour to Gemma, terrified as she was that he might see something of her mother in her. But he didn't, she would have known if he had. She would have seen something in that handsome, cold, implacable face because she was searching for it.

He came towards her and stretched out his hand and Gemma took it and knew that her first impression hadn't misled her. His grip, though firm, was cold and impersonal. His mouth unsmiling.

'I can't say I'm pleased to meet you, young lady, but now that you are here I welcome you.' His voice was deep, almost a gravel in the depth of his throat.

There was no sincerity in the welcome bit and Gemma was hardly surprised; she had been warned he was a complex man. She pressured a smile to her dry lips and said, 'Felipe told me you aren't very happy at having your portrait painted, but I promise you it will be painless.'

He raised a grey streaked brow at that. 'It had better be,' he told her coldly, entirely missing the humour she was trying to inject into the conversation. 'I'm not a vain man and I see no point in having a life-sized replica of myself hanging around for people to stick pins in, but, if Felipe commands it, let it be.'

So he was very aware of his unpopularity and more. His tone was leaden with sarcasm and he then proceeded to throw a dark look in Felipe's direction which was returned with such a positive smirk that Gemma was quite puzzled.

'You won't be disappointed with my work, Señor de Navas——'

'Yes, yes.' He waved a hand dismissively and Gemma bridled at his rudeness. 'Pour me another drink, Felipe.'

'So tell me about yourself?' Agustín surprised her with, then motioned her to sit down, which she didn't do because he was still speaking. 'And I don't want a life history, just tell me how a beautiful woman such as yourself gets to be painting portraits of rich old men such as I.'

'I wouldn't have said you were rich...'

Dear God, she had meant to say old! Her face flushed furiously and her pulse raced so violently that she thought everyone must be aware of it. To her utter surprise Agustín burst out laughing.

'So, I'm old, am I?'

'I'm sorry. I meant to say I wouldn't have said you were old but rich came out instead.'

'Really,' he mused tonelessly. 'Was I supposed to be flattered if you'd got it right?' He nodded his head towards the sofa again and this time Gemma obeyed the silent command and sat down, gratefully. She'd never felt a bigger fool in her life.

'Yes,' Gemma answered honestly, and why not? This man was more than a client—he was her father. Because of that he didn't daunt her, not much anyway. 'If it had come out right I'd have hoped it would have warmed you.'

His eyes registered a swift blaze of anger which was equally swiftly controlled.

'Implying I'm a cold bastard?' he said gruffly.

Gemma inwardly flinched at that. For some reason she got the impression the remark wasn't intended for her, though Agustín's eyes were full on her face.

Felipe stepped forward with the drinks. 'I think that was uncalled for, Agustín. We have a lady in our midst...'

She was right, it hadn't been aimed at her; it had been a bitter aside for Felipe's benefit. Gemma noted the spark of antagonism between them—or was it simply familiarity? She really wasn't very sure about this relationship between them.

'I'm not offended, Felipe, and I'm sure Señor de Navas didn't intend it to offend, but he has a point.' They both looked at her in surprise and with a very forced smile Gemma went on. 'I'm going to paint your portrait, Señor de Navas. I was trying to humour you to relax you, so I could study your features and your bone-structure. If I want to paint the real you I have to see the real you, otherwise my trip out here to your home is a waste of time. You could have sent a photograph and I would have copied it.'

Gemma took the drink Felipe held out to her and gulped at it.

'That would have suited me better,' Agustín stated brittly. 'I have better things to do with my time than sit twiddling my thumbs having my portrait painted.'

She sensed that that also was directed at Felipe. Somehow she sympathised with Agustín. He just didn't want his portrait painted and Felipe had forced it on him to get her down here to Venezuela.

'If you don't want it done I won't do it,' Gemma offered. What did it matter anyway? She didn't need this commission. 'I would hate to impose on your life...'

'How many sessions did you have in mind?' Agustín cut in.

She looked up at him, hating to be intimidated by him towering over her. 'I can't say. It depends how well it goes. I'd like to start with a couple of sessions a day, perhaps an hour in the morning and an hour in the afternoon...' Why was she saying this? She didn't even want to stay.

'Out of the question! I'll fit you in when I can. Felipe will deal with it, as it was his ridiculous idea in the first place,' he told her impatiently. He glanced at his watch. 'If Bianca isn't down in five minutes we'll go in without her. Didn't that damned expensive education of hers teach her punctuality? I have a call to make. Pour Gemma another drink, Felipe.'

He strode from the room, leaving them alone, and Gemma realised that his last order to Felipe was the only time he'd spoken her name and then not directly to her.

'Do you want another drink?'

Gemma shook her head. 'No, thank you. I haven't finished this yet.' She stared at it dismally. Felipe had forewarned her that her father was a difficult man but it hadn't helped. She felt shaken—and what else? Disappointed? So he was a good-looking man; she'd almost anticipated that anyway. Her mother had good taste and she hadn't doubted it stretched to men too. But what a disappointment to find his character didn't level with his looks. Pleasant to look at, he was; pleasant to be with, he wasn't.

'How does he grab you?' Felipe asked rhetorically, refilling his glass. 'By the throat with gloves of tempered steel?'

Gemma smiled, albeit hesitantly. 'He's a...a bit abrasive.'

'That's putting it mildly,' Felipe murmured.

'How do you stand working for him?'

'We are stuck with each other, for better, for worse. Sometimes we irritate the hell out of each other.'

Gemma opened her mouth to speak, but shut it again. She didn't understand these people, certainly didn't understand how they could be stuck with each other for better or worse. If they didn't get on, why didn't Felipe move on? There were a thousand other oil companies he could work for.

A dinner gong sounded, and, taut as her nerves were, she jerked.

Felipe noticed and came and touched her arm. She pulled it away, looking at him venomously. He gave her a look that was so coldly impenetrable that she inwardly flinched.

'Let's go in to dinner before we both get our legs slapped,' he said, trying to humour her. She gave him a frozen look and walked with him out of the room.

The dining-room was positively baronial. She'd seen it before but not this way. The two massive wrought-iron chandeliers glowed over the dining table, which was superbly set. The light on the crystal fragmented into a myriad sparkles. The silver was heavy, antique and priceless as was the beautiful china. A huge candelabrum was the centrepiece with a dozen or so off-white candles burning among the nymphs that danced around them. Shallow bowls of creamy-coloured orchids were distributed among the crystal and the silverware. Gemma wished her state of mind could fully appreciate the beauty of it all.

Agustín stood at the head of the table, waiting for them as they entered the room. 'Sit here, Gemma.' He motioned to the seat to his left and she sat down. 'Felipe, will you have a word with Bianca? I will not tolerate lateness. We dine at nine, she knows that well enough.'

'You have a word with her,' Felipe threw back, taking the seat next to the one Bianca was obviously going to occupy, to Agustín's right. 'She's your guest, not mine.'

Gemma's heart stopped and when it started again she shot a worried glance at both men. Agustín's fury was well controlled, only given away by a tensing of his jaw muscles. Gemma couldn't believe that Felipe could speak to his employer so bluntly, couldn't believe that Agustín didn't bawl him out, couldn't believe that Felipe's cousin was Agustín's guest!

'Where did you train?' Agustín asked Gemma unexpectedly as Maria started to serve the first course, a cold white soup that smelt of garlic and almonds and had green grapes floating in it.

'Goldsmith's...' It was out before she could stop it. The art college her mother had trained at too. Would Agustín remember? After six months with her mother he must have known everything about her. She watched his face, saw a pulse throb at his temple, but wasn't sure if her imagination hadn't spirited it there.

'After I left college,' Gemma went on, 'I studied privately under Cyrus Paget for a year. He's quite famous in Europe...'

'Royal Academy,' Agustín murmured, concentrating on his soup. 'You had a good tutor.'

Gemma's heartbeat quickened. He knew a bit about art. 'Yes, the best.'

'You must be talented for him to take you under his wing.'

'She is,' Felipe said for her. 'I wouldn't have suggested her for the job if I didn't think she was the only one in the world who could make a silk purse out of a pig's ear.'

Gemma froze her eyes to the bowl of soup in front of her. Surely Agustín would hit the roof at that insult? But there was nothing, no reaction whatsoever. Confused? Gemma was.

The next course, '*Chipi chipi*,' Felipe told her across the table, was tiny clams in a rich creamy sauce. Gemma couldn't abide shellfish but was too polite to refuse. She picked at it, finding it wasn't so bad, and managed to finish it as Felipe and Agustín discussed the merits of the orchids that were displayed on the table.

Gemma sipped her wine, a delicious Californian Chardonnay, and when she looked up she caught Agustín studying her as Felipe talked.

For a frightening second Gemma thought he must know and when, as Felipe turned to compliment Maria on the clams, he said quite softly, 'You have beautiful hair,' she was sure he did.

Her hair was identical to her mother's. But no, he couldn't possibly make the connection. Gemma wondered what he would say if she stood up and said, 'I'm the daughter you didn't know you had.' God, it wasn't even an amusing thought. She gulped some more wine.

'Thank you,' she murmured, acknowledging the compliment, somehow knowing it was a genuine one,

not uttered as a flirtatious gesture. How awful if it
had been!

Maria was busy serving marinated beef at the sideboard when suddenly Bianca swept into the dining
hall, her high heels clipping out her arrival on the
tiles.

All eyes were on her, Felipe's tolerant, Agustín's
furious, Gemma's curious.

She looked as lovely as Gemma remembered her,
jet hair, frizzed and wild around her lovely oval face.
Her pure white dress of fine cotton was well-cut, low-
cut and very blatantly sexy.

With a giggle but not an apology for her lateness
on her red lips she threw her arms around Agustín's
neck and hugged him tightly.

Agustín was not amused and unwound her arms
from his neck as if uncoiling a deadly constrictor.

'When are you going to learn some manners,
Bianca...?'

She took absolutely no notice of Agustín as she
launched herself at Felipe, pressing her lips to his
mouth.

'Bianca!' Agustín roared, and this time Bianca
reacted, sharply, sulkily.

She pulled away from Felipe and slumped down in
the chair on Agustín's right and glared across at
Gemma. Their eyes locked and Bianca's recognition
came slowly, unbelievably, as if she was coming out
of a dream—or a nightmare!

Gemma's heart thudded unpleasantly at the realis-
ation that Bianca hadn't known she was here. Mixed
emotions flooded Gemma's mind.

'This is Gemma, Bianca,' Agustín said, calm now
after his irritation at Bianca nearly throttling him. 'She

is here to paint my portrait. You knew we had a
guest—why the hell weren't you down on time? You
get more impossible by the day.'

'If I'd known *she* was going to be the portrait
painter you told me about I wouldn't have come down
at all!' Bianca said slowly and deliberately. She held
Gemma's eyes, coldly, hostilely, hatefully.

'That's quite enough, Bianca,' Felipe said quickly,
but not quickly enough.

Agustín's jet eyes lasered backwards and forwards
to the two women at his table.

'You two know each other?'

Suddenly Gemma was an onlooker, a part of the
proceedings that followed but not really there. Fierce
chills of horror threaded up and down her spine as
Bianca's mouth twisted cruelly.

'Yes, we've met,' she bit out, her dark eyes shot
with slivers of pure hatred, then she turned them on
Agustín and added spitefully, 'She was shacked up
with Felipe in London months ago!'

There was a fearful silence. Gemma looked at
Felipe, whose face was cold and unfeeling. She hated
him for this, hated him to the very soles of her shoes.

'Is this true, Felipe?' Agustín was calm, too calm.

Felipe looked him straight in the face and said
quietly and lethally, 'I don't need to answer to such
an offensively phrased accusation, to you or anyone.'

'Oh, but you do, Felipe,' Bianca whined. 'I'm sure
Tío would like to hear all about it, wouldn't you?'
she delivered pettishly, giving Agustín a sickly-sweet
smile.

Tío! *Tío*! Gemma knew a few Spanish words, *tío*
being one of them—uncle! If Agustín was Bianca's

uncle and Bianca was Felipe's cousin then Agustín
must be Felipe's uncle too...

'Were you or were you not living with Gemma in
London?' Agustín shouted. No calmness now, just
raw anger that raised him instantly to his feet.

Suddenly Felipe was on his feet too and the men
faced each other, their black eyes warring.

'Don't speak to me as if I were still a child, Agustín.
My life is not yours!'

'I made your life! You'd be nothing without me...'

'Grateful as I am, I can survive without you trying
to command the rest of my life!' Felipe roared. 'When
will I get it through to you that I won't bow to your
every wish——?'

'What was this woman in your life?' Agustín
thundered.

Horrified, Gemma waited, sickened by this row that
was raging as if she wasn't there.

'She was my life,' Felipe breathed heavily. 'She still
is,' he added. 'She is the woman I love and the woman
I'm going to marry!'

Gemma's blood ran cold with shock and her mouth
parted to speak but no sound came from her lips.
There was a small sob from Bianca and a vicious
intake of breath from Agustín.

'It's arranged,' Bianca screeched. '*We* are going to
be married, Felipe!'

Gemma thought her heart would stop. She tried to
will her legs to move so she could run from this horror
but they wouldn't be fired into life.

Suddenly Agustín's fist slammed down on the table,
shuddering the flames of the candles, slurping wine
from the crystal glasses.

'Enough!' he roared, his skin dark burgundy with rage. 'How dare you do this to me? How dare you?' He clenched his fists, his eyes not shifting from Felipe's. 'You will not marry the English, Felipe, you marry your cousin——'

'And you and your precious schemes can go to hell where you both belong!' Felipe fired back at him.

Gemma got to her leaden feet then, her head swimming, her stomach lurching dangerously. She wished instant deafness on herself, not wanting to hear another word of this horrible family row.

'Will you excuse me?' she said faintly. 'I don't want to be a part of this.'

'Gemma,' Felipe called, but his voice was in the distance, so far away.

The curving stone stairs were long and tortuous and Gemma thought she would never get to the top of them. She heard someone else call her but didn't heed the cry. Dizzily she flung open her bedroom door and just reached the bathroom in time.

Grasping the edge of the sink, she was violently sick. She felt arms supporting her. Maria. Gemma clung to her, so glad she was there and no one else.

'You all right now?' Maria asked anxiously.

Gemma nodded weakly, tears streaming from her eyes. 'Did you hear, Maria? That terrible row.'

'*Si*, I hear, I hear all, Gemma. The family have the worst rows and that Bianca, she trouble. She make it bad between father and son——'

Red fire flashed before Gemma's eyes. Her grip tightened on Maria's arms.

'Wh . . . what did you say?' Please, God, don't let it be true! 'Father and son?' Gemma croaked disbelievingly.

Maria patted her arm. '*Si*, it's natural for the father and son to fight . . .'

The fire engulfed her, reduced her to ashes in a fiery instant. Gemma crumbled to a heap on the bathroom floor.

CHAPTER SIX

THERE was pain, a deep physical pain, low down in her stomach. Gemma's head swam sickeningly and she was so hot, on fire from her throbbing head to her burning toes.

She felt cool water on her forehead. Slowly she opened her eyes. The fan spun slowly, persistently over the bed. Maria came into focus, hovering over her with a damp face cloth.

'You sick, Gemma. I get Felipe.'

'No!' Gemma cried, grasping the sleeve of Maria's black blouse. 'No, I don't want to see anyone, not yet, not ever!'

Maria looked frightened. 'I should tell Señor de Navas. You faint and you have sickness. You have the pain?'

Gemma nodded, rubbing her stomach, and then she knew what had caused it.

'I shouldn't have eaten the *chipi*, the clams. I don't really like them and seafood doesn't agree with me.'

'*Dios mío*! Is my cooking make you bad?'

'No, Maria, it isn't your cooking, it's me. I'm all right now.'

She sat on the edge of the bed and held her forehead in her hands. She wasn't all right; far from it, the pain in her stomach might be receding but not in her heart. She was trembling from head to toe with shock but she had to pull herself together, she had to!

'I have some powders I make for you but first I get you into bed.'

'Honestly, Maria, I'm much better now. Being sick helped. I just want to sit here and get myself together.' Oh, please go, Gemma inwardly implored. She wanted to be alone, completely alone, for ever!

'I still get the powders,' Maria told her, going to the door.

'Maria, I don't want to see anyone,' she reminded her as she got to the door. She needed time to think, to plan a way out of this awful mess.

'Is too late,' Maria smiled from the doorway, thinking that Felipe was the exception. 'Gemma is sick,' she told him. 'She sick, she faint. I go for the powders.'

Felipe came towards her, his face grey with worry.

'There's nothing to worry about...' Gemma croaked, the anguish in her eyes defying him to touch her.

'There is, you look as white as a sheet...'

'I've been sick. I shouldn't have eaten the clams—they don't agree with me.' The words came out in a feverish rush and she looked away, not able to look into his eyes. This was too soon, this confrontation. She didn't want him here, showing concern, breathing the same air as her.

He leaned down to place a hand on her shoulder and his touch was like a branding iron on her senses. She moved away, quickly, jerkily, standing up and going to the window to put distance between them. Oh, God, he mustn't touch her, not ever again...

'But you fainted,' he persisted.

She jerked her head towards him. 'Was it any wonder?' she cried. 'How dare you do that to me,

use me in your war games with Agustín . . . ?' He must
never know the truth, why she had passed out. The
shock had been too much for her already tormented
mind to cope with. It would never pass, this sickness
and disgust inside her: she had made love to her
own——

'I'm sorry,' Felipe said softly as if he'd just realised
what was wrong with her, 'sorry you got caught up
in our family row.'

'You think an apology will make it all right? You're
sick, Felipe, and I hate you for what you've done.
What vicious, wicked games you play! Torment me,
torment Bianca . . . is there no let-up from you?' She
didn't wait for an answer but blazed on. 'Everything
you have wished for has come true. You have pun-
ished me more than enough but you can't stop. You
bring Bianca here to push me over the edge.' She had
to do this, throw everything at him. It was the only
way to be rid of this terrible feeling inside her.

'Agustín brought Bianca here.'

'You told me yourself she was coming next week.
She was part of the plan to torment me. This week,
next week, what difference?'

'A world of difference,' he told her darkly.

'And what's that supposed to mean?' God, why
was she bothering to ask? She didn't want to know,
didn't care any more what his motives were. Nothing
in her life, past or present or future, mattered any
more.

'In your present state of hysteria I doubt you would
understand.'

'I only understand one thing, Felipe: your bitterness, Agustín's bitterness, Bianca's bitterness. You
are all tarred the same. I'm the pawn in your devious

games, to be used and then cast aside. Great, that
suits me fine. I want out of here anyway!' She had
to go! It was imperative that she leave this very minute.

He came towards her then and Gemma swayed as
if someone had upended the room. He stood so close
to her his breath was warm on her face. 'After last
night, you want out of here?' he drawled coldly.

Nausea rose inside Gemma. A flush careered across
her cheeks. Last night! How could she bear to think
of it? She turned away to gaze dizzily out into the
black night but Felipe took her chin and jerked her
head to face him. 'We made love last night and it had
nothing to do with revenge. I meant what I said
downstairs. You are my life——'

'But you're not mine!' Gemma spat out, so sharply
she fired instant anger to his eyes. His hand fell away
from her chin. 'You said you wanted to marry me,'
she went on, 'and don't you think I know what
spurred that insane proposal? You hate your father
and you used me to stab at him . . .'

She stopped as pain tore at her heart. If only she
had known the truth, that Felipe was the son of
Agustín, none of this would have happened. Their
affair in London would have happened, nothing could
have prevented that, it was destined, but if he had left
things alone and not arranged this commission to get
her here she would never have *known*!

'Why, Felipe!' she screamed in anguish. 'Why didn't
you tell me Agustín was your father?'

His eyes glittered darkly and Gemma waited for his
answer, but knowing that it made no difference. How
could it? But she just wanted to lay the blame anywhere but on her own shoulders. It was his fault, all
his damned fault!

'It was no concern in our life,' he told her.

She shut her eyes in pained sufferance. No concern in our life. Oh, God, from now on she had no life.

'Get out, Felipe,' she said through her teeth. 'Get out of my bedroom. I never want to see you again.'

'But you're going to, *querida*, because we want each other and nothing in this world is going to change that!' he grated, and then he did what she prayed he wouldn't. He gripped her forcibly by her arms and lowered his lips to hers. Shame fired her strength, shame and rage and disgust. She tore herself from his arms, bruising her arms as he tried to hold on to her.

'Go back to Bianca where you belong,' she spat. 'I told you that making love to me would make no difference. You had my body last night but not my heart . . .'

He went still as if he'd been punched so hard that it had knocked the living breath from him. 'You bitch!' he rasped at last, living anger flooding back into his bones and darkening his skin. 'You cold, hard bitch!'

He turned and left her then, slamming the door hard behind him.

Gemma stared at the back of the door. Nervous perspiration poured from her brow and with trembling fingers she wiped the moisture from her face and gazed down at it as if expecting to see her life blood on her fingertips. Slowly she lowered herself into a chair by the window and clutched at her bruised arms and rocked herself to and fro. She stayed that way far into the hot night.

'You still sick, Gemma?' Maria asked the next morning, putting a tray down on the sideboard and sweeping the lace drapes back from the window. 'Felipe he say not to bring you the powders last night, said to leave you to sleep.'

Gemma lay like a corpse in her bed. She'd hardly slept, only a little at dawn. She was exhausted with thinking. She had to leave and this morning if possible.

'Drink this, Gemma,' Maria softly ordered.

Gemma struggled up on to her pillows and feebly took the glass of dissolved powders from Maria. She wished it were strychnine; that was the only answer to this awful mess. She swallowed the draught and her head started to clear almost immediately.

'Señor de Navas, he want you at ten . . .'

'Felipe?' Gemma croaked, looking up at Maria in disbelief. After last night she would have thought he never wanted to see her again.

'No Felipe—Agustín. In his study at ten.'

'It's nearly that now!'

'*Si*, you hurry, he no like you late.'

'I won't be,' Gemma said resolutely, leaping out of bed. So Agustín wanted to see her, did he? To dismiss her from the Villa Verde? Nothing would give her greater pleasure but to accept that dismissal with open arms.

She dressed quickly in a cotton sundress after raking a comb through her hair, smoothing it down with her palms before flying out of her bedroom. If there were any justice in this world Mike would be revving the engines of the plane at this very moment. She ran downstairs, knocked on the study door and walked straight in without waiting for an answer.

He looked no less severe this morning though he was dressed casually enough in light grey trousers and a white short-sleeved shirt. He was seated at his desk and he leaned back in his chair as she walked into the room.

It all hit her then, last night, him and Felipe arguing, Bianca sticking her vicious oar in, Maria's revelations. She felt incredibly sick and shaken and must have looked it because Agustín urged her to sit down. She nearly fell into the chair in front of his desk.

'Maria tells me you ate food that didn't agree with you. Rather a silly thing to do, wasn't it?'

'Perfectly idiotic,' Gemma agreed, her strength and bite rallying.

'I apologise for our behaviour last night. It was unspeakably rude of us and you are a guest in our home.'

Gemma shook her head, a curtain of jet silk caressing her cheek. 'I'm not a guest in your home, señor . . .'

'Please call me Agustín.'

She nodded and went on. 'I came here to do a job and I'm sorry that it didn't work out.'

Apparently he didn't hear her because his next statement came without preamble. 'You had an affair with my son in London. I'd like to hear about it.'

She was surprised; her eyes widened. 'I don't think it has anything to do with you,' she answered quickly. She didn't want to talk about it, to even think about it any more.

He raised a brow. 'Don't you? You have badly interfered with the plans I had for my son, I think that has everything to do with me.'

'But nothing to do with me,' Gemma told him resolutely. She didn't need this, to be cross-examined as if she were a criminal. She had done nothing wrong, not knowingly anyway. 'You have nothing to fear from me. I'm not going to marry your son. I plan to leave as soon as possible.'

He awarded her a cynical smile for her intention. 'You were summoned here to paint my portrait and that is precisely what you will do.'

Gemma's mouth parted in shock. No, not this, not strong-arm tactics from him, she'd had enough of that from Felipe.

'You don't understand——'

'You were commissioned to paint my portrait and you will.'

'I wish to withdraw from the contract,' she told him defiantly. She couldn't stay. If she lost a lifetime of commissions over this she would do it to be free. 'You don't want it done and I don't want to do it——'

'Because I refuse to allow you to marry my son?'

'I think Felipe is old enough to make his own decisions, but that isn't the point. I don't want to marry him, with or without your permission.' Of course he couldn't know how sickeningly impossible it was anyway. Sickeningly impossible, that was the sum of it all.

He stood up, tall and proud, and slowly came round the side of the desk to be closer to her. He perched on the edge of the desk. 'That's twice you've denied wanting to marry him. That surprises me. Most women would give their soul to the devil to be married to my son. Do you love him?'

The question was so unexpected that Gemma nearly choked. Quickly she composed herself and forced an answer, a very inadequate one she thought but it was the best she could do.

'That is my business.'

'You *are* in love with him.'

She couldn't stand any more of this. If she didn't
need his permission for Mike to fly her out of here
she would storm from the room. 'I find your questions impertinent,' she told him, unable to mask the
hurt in her voice.

'I'm sorry, I didn't mean to offend you.' He said
it so softly that Gemma's heart jerked. Softness was
a characteristic she hadn't expected from him, hadn't
thought it was one he was capable of.

'You...you don't offend me. I...I understand your
curiosity.'

'Yes, I am curious,' he murmured. 'You interest
me.'

Gemma's nerves were suddenly on red alert. She
didn't want him probing into her life. It would be so
easy to let something slip, some little thing that would
connect her to her mother. She went for diversionary
tactics. 'You interest me too.' He looked surprised at
that. 'Why do you feel it your duty to arrange your
son's marriage?'

His eyes narrowed warningly. 'I now find *your*
questions impertinent, but perhaps I owe you some
sort of explanation. You must have heard the expression "stick to your own kind". I want Felipe to
marry one of his own kind.'

'Why?' Gemma asked bluntly.

'Because it is as it should be. You are of a different
culture and do not know our ways. Felipe will be safer
with a wife of his own culture.'

Gemma couldn't agree more. Culture as in exper-
imentally grown bacteria! 'An arranged marriage? I
thought that went out with the Charleston. Was your
marriage arranged?' She was posing this daring
question for her mother, she realised. Perhaps trying

to salvage some sort of human understanding out of this twisted mess.

'Yes, it was,' he admitted.

'And . . . and you were lucky enough to love her?' Why was she doing this? Her mother had loved this man, still did; why was she searching for something from him that might hurt her?

'Love isn't necessary to make a good marriage; it can come later,' he told her brittly.

But it didn't for you, Gemma wanted to say. She could tell by his tone that it hadn't worked for him. She watched him as he walked away from her to sit at his desk again and she saw bitterness in his face and wondered at it.

'If you feel well enough I'd like you to start today.'

'The . . . the portrait,' Gemma husked unbelievably. 'But I . . . I don't want to do it. I mean . . . it's impossible now.'

'Nothing is impossible. Difficult, perhaps, but never impossible.'

'But it isn't fair, not fair to me after what has happened,' Gemma protested hotly. 'You can't expect me to stay on here after last night.' Especially after last night and what I learnt, she wanted to cry. But how impossible to be able to tell anyone. What a terrible secret she was burdened with for the rest of her days.

His eyes narrowed again. 'I will have a word with Bianca. She won't trouble you, if that is what you are afraid of. As for you and Felipe, the problem is yours. You started it and you will have to sort it out as best you can. Be back here at two this afternoon to start the portrait. Now if you'll excuse me I have work to do.'

Gemma stood up, quite prepared to argue her case, but with an upward, dismissive glance at her he lifted the phone. Gemma turned on her heel and stormed from the room.

This was impossible. First Felipe had scuttled her plans to leave, now Agustín. She raked a frustrated hand through her hair and wandered outside. She wouldn't stay. She was damned adamant about that.

She found Felipe in the orchid garden. 'I'd like you to have a word with your father,' she started when he turned to look at her. He was re-potting a delicate sapphire-blue orchid that had split out of its pot, his strong tanned hands a sharp contrast to the pale exotic blooms he handled so tenderly. His hands, so gentle at times, so tantalising, so exciting . . . She bit hard on her bottom lip to stop the rush of blood to her head.

'For what reason?' he asked tersely.

'I can't stay here, you know I can't!' He didn't know why, though, and he would never know the real reason she wanted to put an ocean between them.

'Agustín has taken to you. He wants the portrait and you will paint it.' He went on with his re-potting as if she were nothing but an irritating fly hassling the progress of his work.

'I'm not interested in how Agustín feels about me, or the portrait. I just want to get out of all your lives.'

'But you can't. I want you, Agustín wants you——'

'Why should you want me, Felipe?' she burst out bitterly. 'More punishment? Or perhaps the tactics have changed. Are you tired of Bianca and want to use me to be rid of her?'

'I don't need to use you——'

'No, because you want her. So you just want me around to wind me up further and to taunt your own father. You're wasting your time with me and I suspect you're wasting you're time with Agustín as well. He appears to be a very powerful and strong-willed man.'

'And so am I,' he told her tightly.

'Look, I'm honestly not interested in your emotional battles. I find you both as slippery and as twisted as boa constrictors and I don't care if you throttle the life out of each other but leave me out!'

He smiled, and that angered Gemma more.

'You really aren't taking all this seriously, are you?' she stormed.

'I took our night of love seriously enough...'

Her eyes blinked in suffering. 'Shut up! All this is your fault and if you were any sort of a man you would put it to rights.'

'If I was any sort of man I'd thrash you to an inch of your life.'

'That's the Latin American way, is it? Well, this isn't the eighteenth century, though no one would know it round here. The Villa Verde is positively feudal compared to what goes on in normal civilisation.'

'Different worlds, Gemma,' he snapped harshly. 'My God, what a lucky escape we've had. Marriage to you would be intolerable.'

'Ah, so you admit you don't want to marry me and that stupid proposal was a ploy to get your father's back up? Great, your words are music to my ears,' Gemma gushed sarcastically. 'Now you can think to your future with Bianca—marriage to her is sure to be a bed of barbed wire which no doubt your sadistic temperament will welcome.'

'I'll never know. I have no intentions of marrying her,' he told her levelly, refusing to be aroused by her gibes.

'Are you sure? I got the distinct impression it was Daddy's wish.'

She had got to him and his eyes raked her derisively. 'You wear bitchiness well.'

'On you, cruelty suits!'

Their eyes locked in silent war. Once they had been lovers—now they were enemies, and thank God, Gemma thought. This was the only way, to refuel their bitterness towards each other.

He turned back to his orchids. 'Much as I wish you out of my life, I can't do anything about it. Agustín wants you here and Agustín gets what he wants.'

Gemma folded her arms across her chest. 'That sounds like a contradiction of what you've just said.'

'Marrying Bianca?' His mouth twisted into a wry smile. 'You have a point. Shall I rephrase that? Agustín *occasionally* gets what he wants. And the longer I am in your company, the more marriage to Bianca appeals.'

Gemma sunk her nails into her own flesh. Some time ago his words would have broken her heart. Now she had to suffer them and accept that they were a possibility. Felipe married to Bianca, better than she married to Felipe, her half-brother!

'Please talk to Agustín,' Gemma gently implored. 'I can't bear to stay here. You can arrange for me to leave today. You know it is for the best.'

The depth and feeling of her plea had Felipe swinging to her with such concern in his eyes that she wanted to run to him and beg him to tell her this was a terrible nightmare and soon she would wake up and all would be sweet and well with the world.

She stiffened desperately as he closed in on her, his dark eyes searching hers for something she was forbidden to give him.

'Don't, Felipe,' she uttered, terror stiffening her spine. 'Please don't touch me.'

'What would happen if I did, Gemma?' he said threateningly. 'Would we come out of this nightmare and love each other again, the way we did the other night?'

So he recognised the nightmare too, but for such different reasons. Did he still love her? It sounded as if he did, and for once in her life she wished he didn't.

As he stood watching her, searching her misty brown eyes for an answer, she was tempted. Oh, so tempted to tell him the truth, that she had loved him so deeply and completely and she still did but she wasn't free any more and nor was he. Their love was wrong, forbidden, and could never be and would never be again as long as she drew breath. Living with the past and the horrendous thoughts of what they had unknowingly committed would be traumatic enough, but their future? Their future was non-existent.

With tears in her eyes and her throat raw with pain she mouthed husking words she prayed would end this torment. 'I don't love you, Felipe. Maybe that was why I didn't call you in New York. I didn't care enough to put myself out. We had an affair and that was all——'

'We were good in bed, is that what you're saying?' he interjected quietly, and she lowered her eyes in such deep shame that she wanted to die with the pain of it all.

What had they done? This was a result of the folly
of loving a stranger, not knowing who he was or caring
at the time. He'd picked her up at her own exhibition . . . a pick-up? No, not that . . . they had loved
each other, openly, willingly, without thought that . . .
Oh, God, what punishment, what torment for their
urgent impulses. He was her brother...she his sister...

'Yes, that's what I'm saying, and that's all it was,
nothing more,' Gemma husked back coldly.

A nerve pulsed at his throat and for a long moment
his eyes never left hers and then he turned away from
her and Gemma knew she'd had the last biting cruel
words that were to end this torment once and for all.

'You pack, Gemma? I no understand.'

Gemma jumped and swung to face Maria, hoping
she didn't notice her red-rimmed eyes, her blotchy
skin. She had cried herself senseless when she had got
to her room and a puffy face was the result. She didn't
feel better for it, though. She still ached all over as
if she had been rugby-tackled by her own emotions.

'I'm leaving, Maria,' Gemma told her grimly as she
snapped shut the catches of her case and stretched her
aching back.

'I no understand,' Maria repeated plaintively from
the other side of the bed. 'Señor de Navas, he send
me for you. Say you are late.'

Damn Felipe! He hadn't been to see Agustín after
all and she had thought he would. She had convinced
herself that after their painful confrontation in the
orchid garden he would want to end this agony and
be rid of her?

'Where is Felipe?'

'The... the stables with Bianca. They go to ride.'
Maria admitted it so hesitantly that Gemma couldn't
help but smile, albeit grimly. Felipe had wasted little
time. Horses they had in common, no doubt, and
many other things that weren't forbidden to them...

'OK,' Gemma murmured resolutely. So she had no
choice but to stay. She doubted Agustín would take
any notice of any further pleas for her release of the
contract. And Felipe... had he more punishment in
mind for her? He'd made no attempt to secure her
freedom and the reason why wasn't quite clear but no
doubt he would make it so before very long. He was
out riding with Bianca. Trying to wound her more or
perhaps he simply preferred his cousin's company?
She didn't know or care because it was all for the best.
Meanwhile she had a portrait to paint, and it seemed
there was no way she could get out of it. With Felipe
back in the arms of his cousin it might just be possible
to paint the quickest portrait of her life.

'OK,' Gemma repeated. She was going to cope. She
had the strength now and the fight. 'Could you send
Pepe up for my case, Maria? If I must stay, I won't
stay in this house...'

'I no understand...' Maria eyes were wide.

Gemma smiled. 'It's all right, Maria, there isn't
much to understand. I'm moving into the studio, that's
all. Agustín can have forty fits for all I care but at
least I'll be out of everyone's way.'

Maria gazed at her in awe for a few seconds and
then she shook her head. 'You crazy, you know!'

'Yes, Maria, I very probably am!' Gemma conceded on a deep sigh.

CHAPTER SEVEN

'YOU'RE late, and I would have thought you would have learnt by now that I can't tolerate unpunctuality!' Agustín blazed at her when she eventually got to his study.

Gemma wanted to laugh, hysterically. Everything was going from bad to worse. They were all quite mad, the whole de Navas family.

Gemma stood her ground, across the desk from Agustín. 'I don't want to paint you. I want to leave, but——'

'And do you want a career to go back to? Because you won't have by the time I've finished with you!'

More threats. This man and his son might have their differences but in temperament they were identical. Bullying, cruel, selfish chauvinists! She didn't doubt that either of them could destroy her career.

Taking an enormous breath, Gemma cooled herself. 'Will you let me finish? I don't want to stay, but as you won't let me leave I'll stay on my own terms——'

'Don't try and bargain with me——'

'No bargain, I assure you. I know what I want and I aim to have it,' Gemma told him severely. 'You might cow your family, Agustín, but not me.'

She could almost laugh at that. She *was* his family, one of his own, and that was why she was standing up to him. It was all about genes. She had some of his.

'I was summoned here to do a job and I'll do it but I want nothing to do with any of you on a personal basis. I want to move into the studio, to work there, sleep there, eat there——'

'What the hell are you talking about?' Agustín sliced in sharply. 'What studio?'

The studio was Agustín's personal folly, the place he had created for a woman he had loved. No one had dared approach it till Felipe and now Gemma knew why he had done it, not to make her work any easier but to hit back at Agustín. For a swift second her sympathies lay with this man before her. He looked bewildered and hurt.

Gemma nodded towards the double doors, locked since the day she had finished Christina's portrait. 'I'm sorry,' she murmured, 'I really am. I did a picture of Christina for Maria while I was waiting for you to return from Maracaibo. I did it in the studio because there was nowhere else for me to work. It's too dark in the house and...' Her voice trailed away. She waited for the outburst of fury she was sure was hanging suspended from his lips.

Agustín stared at her, his face pale. 'Why did you apologise?' he said quietly.

He hadn't exploded with rage and to Gemma that said it all. He was more hurt than anything. If that had been Felipe's intention he had succeeded. Oh, what evil games they all played with each other's emotions.

'Because I guessed what it meant to you,' Gemma told him gently. 'Someone told me the rumours, why you had built the place...'

He held up his hand to silence her and slowly shook his head in disbelief. He didn't want to hear any more.

'Make all the necessary arrangements with Maria. I think in the circumstances it would be better if you did move in there.' He looked up at her. 'You've had a traumatic time here, haven't you?'

He was shrewd and had guessed exactly how she felt about Felipe. Gemma held his gaze, father and daughter for an instant bonded, though she wasn't sure why she had that impression. 'It hasn't been easy,' she admitted, but wasn't about to admit more. She tilted her chin proudly. 'If I get settled in today, perhaps we could start first thing in the morning, if that's all right with you.'

He nodded. 'Perfectly acceptable.'

'What's going on here?' Felipe thundered as he strode into the studio later.

'I've moved in,' Gemma told him stiffly. 'What does it look like?'

She hung the last of her dresses on the pole Pepe had rigged up for her across an alcove. A makeshift wardrobe, fine for the little time she was going to be here. Maria had put linen on the day-bed and towels in the tiny bathroom and stocked the kitchen with tea and coffee. She had everything she needed.

'And what's the point of that?'

'To keep as far away from you as possible.'

'Don't be damned childish, Gemma. None of this is necessary.'

'It is, seeing as you didn't have a word with your father about me leaving.'

'I did, but he was adamant about you staying.'

Gemma snapped shut her case and slid it in the corner. So he had wanted to be rid of her. She should be hurt but instead she was afraid. If he hadn't got his way with his father he would take it out on someone, and at the moment she was the prime target. Her nerves couldn't take any more. All she wanted in life at this moment was to be left to execute this portrait in peace.

'Yes, he really does want his portrait painted after all,' she murmured.

'I doubt that. I believe he wants you here to rub salt into my wounds.'

'Well, you would think that, wouldn't you?' she retorted. 'It's that nasty streak in you that keeps manifesting itself like the spirit of evil.'

'I know Agustín better than you do...'

Hands on hips, Gemma defied him across the studio floor. 'I don't think you know him at all!'

He gave her a slow smile, a knowing smile. 'I do believe you've bewitched each other. You sticking up for him and him allowing you to violate his lover's sanctum. Be careful, sweet one, he'll bewitch you into his bed if you're not careful.'

She was too far away to deliver a deadly blow for that horrific suggestion. But he didn't know, she reminded herself, though that didn't soften the insult. She unclenched her fists at her side and swallowed her fury.

'After you, Satan himself would be welcome,' she told him flintily.

The distance between them miraculously disappeared. His fingers of iron gripped her wrist fiercely, shaking her limp hand in front of her face.

'If I ever thought...'

She balled her fist. 'Thought what? That I was interested in your father? You're despicable, do you know that? Now let go of me before I scream and have your *bewitched* father on our necks.'

He thrust her fist back at her as if it were shoddy goods at sale time. Silently she rubbed away the pain and her eyes locked hatefully with his. This was the base level they had come to, throwing hurtful insults at each other, each vying for the most violent thrust. But it was for the best, she reminded herself. While they were verbally lashing each other nothing else was likely to happen.

'You're in my bedroom,' she informed him stonily. 'And only people I like get in a second time.'

'Like my father, perhaps?'

Contemptuously Gemma held his eyes. She thought she had experienced every emotional pain in the book, suffered every last indignity that life could bestow on anyone. This was something new, to be accused of wanting her father. She gave Felipe no credit for not knowing that the man he accused her of wanting was her father as well. So, if he insisted on thinking that way, who was she to deny it? She wanted to punish him, no matter what cost to her own dignity.

She shrugged her shoulders dismissively. 'He's a very attractive man——'

His hand shot up to her chin, gripped it so viciously her mouth parted with pain and shock. 'If I ever thought...' he repeated. Suddenly his eyes glazed darkly with the tempting fullness of her lips and then his mouth crashed punishingly against hers, grinding hard and agonisingly till she tasted her own blood. Horror was the worst feeling of all. It shot sickeningly from her stomach to her head, spinning it crazily. Desperately she wrenched her mouth from his and he laughed.

'Now I know what it's like to kiss a rabid vixen!'

'And now I know what it's like to be kissed by Mickey Mouse!' she screamed back at him.

He was laughing as he strode out of the door of the studio, not with mirth but with a satanic rumble that promised more punishing torment. It left Gemma shaking with fear but not the fear he had intended. Disgust powered her hand to rub furiously at her mouth.

'If I had my way I'd have you sitting in your shirt-sleeves tending your orchids. I'm sure you'd feel more relaxed.'

Agustín laughed. 'I don't think the boardroom would appreciate that. Do I look so stiff, then?' He adjusted the collar of his light grey suit as if by easing it it would relax the whole of him.

'You did at first,' Gemma smiled, mixing some cobalt blue and burnt sienna on her palette.

'It's not easy, you know.' He shifted uncomfortably on the straight-backed chair she had him sitting on, in a formal pose which his position on the board of his oil company demanded.

'I do know.' Gemma laughed. 'I did some modelling at art school and found it agonising to sit for so long in one position. I really sympathise.'

She stood back from the easel and with a brush between her teeth made a few adjustments to the canvas with her thumb. It was going well, better than she had ever anticipated. The first session had been stiff and formal and they'd been ill at ease with each other. Now, towards the end of the fourth, they had both settled and relaxed.

'Stretch your legs and I'll make some coffee and then I'd like to do another half-hour if you can bear it.'

Agustín stood up and stretched lazily then walked over to the canvas as he did after every session and studied her work, rubbing his chin and occasionally squinting his dark eyes.

Gemma flashed curious glances at him as she put the coffee jug on the small cooker top. She was always interested in people's reactions to seeing themselves on canvas, Agustín's more than anyone. He was her father, and painting his portrait was having a strange effect on her emotions. Every brush stroke was revealing a little bit more of him, on the canvas and to herself. Here, in this studio, he was different. The rough edges of his temperament had smoothed away. Their conversations had at first been stilted but now they came easily, sometimes not at all, but that didn't matter; silence too showed an ease between two people.

Gemma poured two coffees. She liked him, she realised, and suspected he liked her. The feeling was good.

'Does Felipe ever come here?' he asked unexpectedly as he took the coffee-cup she held out to him. He'd loosened his tie at his throat and removed his jacket, and now he stood leaning back against the studio sink. She wondered what Felipe would think of his father now if he saw him. He was hardly the cold, hard bastard he'd labelled him.

'No,' Gemma answered calmly. 'He's too occupied with Bianca to bother coming here. You should be happy about that.'

'But you're not?'

She smiled at him. 'Six months ago I thought my world had come to an end when Felipe walked out on me. I recovered and I'll recover again.'

'You're a strong girl,' he told her, making it sound like a compliment. 'And why did Felipe walk out on you?'

'I . . . I don't know, but he went to New York with Bianca.'

His eyes narrowed, remembering. 'Yes, I summoned them both . . .' Gemma frowned. 'They are my only beneficiaries and there were some company papers to go over.'

Felipe should have told her that; instead he had led her to believe . . . What did it matter now? If he had told her the truth she would have accepted it and they would probably be married now. She gulped at her coffee, a crushing feeling in her chest powering the heat to her face at the thought. No matter how much space she gave to it, no matter how hard she reasoned that what was done was done, she would never get over the fact that Felipe was her half-brother and they had been lovers.

'In time Bianca will make him a good wife,' Agustín told her as if he thought he owed her an explanation. 'She is young yet, like a colt, but he will soon break her in and tame her. She is South American like him and it's always best to stick to your own.' His look was a meaningful reminder of a previous conversation on the subject.

Hurt was beyond her but she could smile at that remark now. 'Is that why you gave up the European woman you loved to marry a woman your father picked for you?' She knew she was riding a knife-edge with that question and she didn't even know for sure if he truly had loved her mother, but this studio was here so his feelings must have been very powerful.

He smiled. 'After all this time,' he mused, 'and still the gossip goes on.'

'You built this studio for her,' she persisted, afraid that that was all she was going to get from him. 'It's a constant reminder to everyone so the rumours go on and one day they will be legend. Didn't your wife object to all this?' She raised her eyes to encompass the airy studio.

'My wife thought it amusing and didn't lose an opportunity to throw it in my face.'

She knew him well enough to know that the tensing of his shoulder muscles meant he was controlling his anger.

'I think we had better get on,' he suggested stonily, and Gemma knew she wouldn't get any more out of him today. She wished their conversation hadn't taken that line because his facial muscles had set determinedly and unless he relaxed the next half-hour was going to be a waste of time.

Gemma knew their routine now and worked her way round it. Felipe and Bianca rode for a couple of hours in the early morning then swam and later, while Bianca sunbathed or painted her nails or hassled Mike the pilot, who seemed to spend a lot of time just hanging around waiting for someone to go somewhere, Felipe worked in the study. They lunched on the terrace and then Bianca slept and Felipe returned to the study to work.

So Gemma fitted a swim in before them and ate lunch in the studio between her morning and afternoon sessions with Agustín. She took the rest of her exercise, wandering the gardens, when no one was around. She avoided them all as if they suffered from some terminal virus.

Maria and Christina popped in to see her and brought her meals, but never when Agustín was there, and all in all everything was working out well.

'I think it's about time you came to your senses and stopped avoiding us.'

Gemma, who'd been on her tenth length of the pool, trod water, clutched at the rail with one hand and swept her wet hair from her face with the other.

She narrowed her eyes against the sun and looked up at Felipe squatting on his haunches by the pool. He wasn't smiling. It had been three days since she had seen him and he looked gaunter than when she had first arrived at the Villa Verde. Bianca must be wearing him ragged.

'Where's Bianca?' Gemma asked, striving for normality. It occurred to her that Felipe probably knew her daily routine as accurately as she knew his.

'Do you care?'

'No, just passing the time of day.' She pushed off from the side and got back to her lengths. Felipe slowly paced next to her.

'I think you should join us for dinner tonight.'

'I think not,' puffed Gemma.

'Why are you being so awkward?'

'Why are you being so persistent?'

She stopped at the end of the pool. She couldn't carry on this conversation and swim at the same time and it was obvious he wasn't going to go away. His hand reached down to her and she took it, forcing casualness into the situation, and he hauled her out.

Felipe bent down, picked up her towel from a lounger and scooped it around her shoulders.

'Thank you,' she murmured, taking a step away from him.

'Agustín says the portrait is coming along splendidly. I'll pop in and take a look at it some time.'

'Don't bother. You'll see enough of it when it's finished. Now, if you'll excuse me, I'd like to get showered and changed before your father's next session.'

He caught her arm and swung her back to him. She didn't know what his intention was but she was ahead of him whatever.

'Don't touch me, Felipe! It wouldn't do for Bianca to see us together, nor your father, come to that.'

'Trying to instigate a bit of intrigue, are you?' he said coldly, his jet eyes raking her, sending a sliver of ice down her spine.

'No, but you obviously are. It was *you* who touched *me*! Now let go of my arm.'

'I'd rather not,' he said, gripping her arm tighter. 'I rather like the feel of you trembling in my grip.'

'Shuddering, you mean,' she said sweetly. Though it came out sarcastically it was heavy with the truth. Every time she thought of what they had done, their intimacies, their love, a shudder of dread and fear shook through her.

He dropped her arm as if it was on fire. 'You're enjoying this, aren't you?'

'The sun, the swim, yes, very much.'

'You know what I mean,' he growled. 'Don't play games with me, Gemma. It makes me very angry.'

'Good, I'm glad I can so easily arouse your wrath.
I take great pleasure in getting back at you for what
you've done to me.'

'Refusing to eat with us and avoiding us is very
childish.'

'I won't argue with that. If you can't beat 'em, join
'em! But if I lived to be a couple of hundred I'll never
match the depth of the de Navases' childishness.'

'You've surpassed it, sweet one. Even Bianca is
showing more maturity than you at the moment.'

'Well, that's saying something, isn't it?' Gemma
sliced back. 'I was always under the impression she
nursed the maturity of a tadpole!' Gemma shrugged.
'Have fun in the stagnant pond of each other's
emotions.'

'Oh, we are,' he laughed cruelly before she turned
away. 'Bianca is suddenly very compromising, thanks
to you.'

Gemma turned back to him just long enough to
throw him a look of disgust. So she was the teaser,
after all, brought in by Felipe to make Bianca see what
she was missing. Had it all been necessary; surely the
girl was already besotted with her cousin? She turned
away from him, and, pulling the robe tightly round
her, walked away. She didn't care a damn anyway, she
told herself as she broke into a trot when she was out
of sight of him. She ran through the cypresses and
round the villa to the sanctuary of the studio. They
all deserved each other—let the devil rot them.

She stood under the shower and found she was
trembling with a mixture of anger and bitter sadness.
How had it all come to this? The rage, the hurting,
the lashing at each other till their emotions took on
the texture of rusted wire wool. Why couldn't he just

leave her alone to get on with her work and then leave her alone to get on with the rest of her life?

A cry of shock caught in her throat as suddenly the shower curtain was stripped aside. If Felipe had been standing there with a knife in his hand ready to emulate Norman Bates in *Psycho* she couldn't have been more shocked.

'What the hell do you think you're doing, scaring me like that?' she croaked. She didn't know which fear superseded the other, fear of death by kitchen knife or fear of Felipe reaching out and touching her nakedness.

His hand came up and twisted off the shower tap and suddenly the silence was terrifying. Then he leaned on the tiles and let his eyes wander relentlessly over her wet, naked body.

Instantly she recognised the arousal in their black depths. A glint of silver, a flash of fiery red and she knew why he was there.

'No, Felipe.' Her words were a whisper in the wind. She lunged at the shower curtain, clutched at it and lashed it around her body. If he touched her, just reached out and tore it from her, she would die.

'No, Felipe,' he echoed mockingly and his hand rose terrifyingly and smoothed a wisp of wet hair from her forehead. 'You mean yes, don't you, *querida*?'

Oh, God, she didn't! Once, but not now, not ever! His fingers caressed the droplets of water from her cheeks, slow, sensual strokes that aroused treacherous thoughts in her mind and body. With the knowledge she possessed, could he still arouse that desperate need inside her? Was it possible she still wanted him, still longed for his touch? The trauma of that thought sickened her till her head swam and she fought it desperately. It was too much to handle, too much for a mind to cope with. In pain and confusion she weakly brought her hand up to push his from her face.

'How easily I can arouse you,' he mocked. 'You struggle to hate me but it is impossible. I struggle to hate you and that is equally impossible. So what is the matter, sweet one?'

Miserably, hopelessly, she shook her head and lowered her eyes. At this moment she knew nothing, even her own name eluded her. She was going mad, losing her reasoning, losing her mind.

His hand moved back to her flaming cheeks and fearfully she grasped his hand, twisted it away from her, her nails biting forcefully into his flesh.

'When will you get it into your mind that I don't want you, Felipe?' she husked drily. She forced herself to look at him, the ultimate in exorcism. It was the only way to do it. Face it, he had said and she was doing just that. Facing the man she illicitly loved, facing the man she knew could never be her own and facing her own disgust and revulsion at what had passed between them. She had loved him, given him her body and soul and now she knew what real torment meant. Ironic that Felipe had willed it on her, but he couldn't know the depth of all she was suffering now.

'And when will you get it into your mind that you are fighting a losing battle, *querida*? It won't go away, you know. The longing for each other——'

'Wrong!' she almost screamed, her eyes ablaze, her face flushed. It had to go away, it simply had to! 'I don't want you any more, Felipe. Your punishment was based on the theory that I cared for you, and

without that the torment doesn't exist. I don't want
you, I don't care for you and no matter what you
threaten you can't do any more damage than you
already have.'

'Can't I?' he mocked, his eyes narrowing threateningly. 'Whether you care for me or not is immaterial.
You can hate me down to your fragile little bones but
one caress and I can melt those bones. I can reach
out and touch you now and the fire will be there, as
hot as ever. You can't deny your body's needs, sweet
one; you can't switch off what powers your sexuality.'

I can, she thought frantically. But she couldn't say
it. To voice her denial would be a challenge to him,
a challenge he would take up just to prove her wrong.
If he did touch her, simply reach out and smooth his
sensuous fingers over any erogenous zone on her flesh
that he wished to name, how would she react? Would
she feel the revulsion she ought to feel or would she
be faced with some terrible dilemma of need that
overpowered her reasoning of right and wrong?
Wasn't what had passed between them enough to cope
with without this treacherous feeling that she *might*
not be able to cope if he put her to the test?

'Agustín will be here in a moment,' she told him,
praying it would be enough to spur him on his way.
Fool. Was she mad? Since when had any threat, disguised or otherwise, rocked Felipe's world?

His eyes hardened. 'Is this what this coy little
charade is all about—showering for your new lover?'

Gemma tightened the shower curtain around her,
twisting the fabric till her fingers whitened. They were
on her lips, like lemmings poised over the precipice,
the words of truth that would shatter three lives if she
let them go. In her mind she said them and pictured
the revulsion that would mar his handsome features.

It would kill him. This proud, arrogant, cruel man would die of shame and disgust if she told him she was Agustín's daughter and he had made love to his own half-sister. And Agustín... Oh, God...these two proud, fiery Latins... They would never know. No matter what she had to suffer, they must never know.

Gemma said nothing. Though she knew her confession would end Felipe's torment once and for all, she couldn't do it. He could drive her to the edge of her sanity and beyond, but she would never, never tell him her terrible secret.

'Answer me, Gemma. Is it my father you want?'

She moved then, furiously pushed past him, ripping the shower curtain down in her haste to get away from him. She grabbed for a towel and flung it round her in place of the curtain. There was nowhere to run to! Her eyes flew round the open studio. She turned and faced him, defied him with the cold brutality of her eyes.

'Leave me alone, Felipe! Stop pestering me! Just get out of my life!'

He didn't even look surprised at her vicious outburst. Even in the worst of her fury he didn't take her seriously. Slowly he came towards her, each step a bleeding wound stabbing at her heart and soul. She stiffened as he stopped in front of her, a knowing smile maliciously twisting the corners of his mouth.

'So you don't deny it. You simply scream at me to leave you alone.' He shook his dark head. 'My father and I might drive each other to distraction at times, but he wouldn't sink so low as to take my woman.'

'I'm not your woman!' Her voice came from somewhere dark and treacherous inside her. It wasn't her voice but somehow she had spirited it to her lips. She

couldn't take much more of this. She felt the fight
going from her and knew that if he kept on she would
blurt the truth. Somehow she rallied a sliver of
strength. 'And I never will be!' she added vehemently
because she knew it to be true.

His eyes raked her dangerously. 'You will be
whatever I wish you to be.'

Suddenly his hand snaked out to the towel held
protectively round her. It was whisked away in a blink
of the eye and Gemma stood naked in front of him,
nothing but cold fear glazing her eyes.

For an instant she saw something in his eyes she
didn't understand. Almost as if he'd recognised her
fear and acknowledged it within him. Then it was gone
and they narrowed warningly.

'Just remember one thing. I know that body better
than you know it yourself. I can control it like no
other man and don't you forget it!' He smiled suddenly and a pulse of triumph throbbed on his jawline.
'You see, *querida*, even my searching eyes can arouse
you.'

Further shame and humiliation flooded her. She had
no control over her own mind, let alone her body. He
only had to cast his jet eyes over her and she betrayed
herself, afraid or not.

Gemma's hands came up to clasp over her breasts,
the breasts that had swelled, their peaks engorged as
he feasted his eyes on her.

His hands shot to hers and he wrenched them away
from herself and held them up so he could take his
fill of her.

'You tremble, sweet one,' he drawled lazily, knowingly, 'not shudder as you claim to do at my touch.'
He let go of her hands but they stayed where they

were, half above her head, as if he was holding a loaded gun to her chest. She was frozen in time, unable to move for the paralysis that gripped her. He grazed the backs of his fingers down over the soft swell of her breasts, circled a persistent thumb round her dark, lust-swollen nipples.

She knew the pain of real torment in that guilt-ridden moment. The torment of her own mind. She closed her eyes to the man she shouldn't love but she could never close her mind to her own shame. It flooded her, drowned out what little there was left of her sanity. She still desired him. The thought was too painful to sustain and in sheer desperation she fought it and blocked it out of her reasoning.

The pressure suddenly stopped and she fluttered open her eyes and gazed up at Felipe. Slowly he took her hands and gently lowered them.

'You see the power I have?' he husked. 'Don't you ever forget it, *querida*, don't you ever forget it!'

He turned and left her standing naked in the stifling studio, pearls of perspiration clustered on her feverish brow. Numbly Gemma stared after him and then her hand came up to clutch over the sob that blurted from her mouth. She reached for the towel he had flung away from her and buried her face in it. She sobbed hysterically into the pile, biting and tearing at the loops, trying to abate her anger and shame. It was useless! It would never go away! She hated herself, hated herself more than she could ever hate him. She had lost control... Dear God... She opened her tear-gritted eyes and stared at the half-finished portrait of her father. He had witnessed her total degradation.

CHAPTER EIGHT

'WHAT are you doing in here?' Gemma asked, her heart thudding nervously. Why should Bianca make her nervous? Why did the sun rising every morning make her nervous? She was a bundle of ragged nerves and had been since the day she realised she still desired Felipe. She still wasn't sure how she'd got through the days; they had just merged into a foggy bank of work and avoiding him once again. But distancing herself from the whole family had seemed to work. No one had bothered her till now!

'I came to see how my uncle's portrait was progressing. He seems so impressed with it, I thought I'd come and see what all the silly fuss was about.' She wrinkled her nose at the canvas. 'Of course, I know nothing about art and wouldn't know if it was good or bad.'

'I'd leave it to the experts, then,' Gemma murmured under her breath, moving across the studio to get her brushes together for Agustín's session. He was due any minute.

'He looks almost human,' Bianca uttered.

'He is human,' Gemma told her, lining up her oils.

'I suppose you think you know him just because you're involved with him so intimately. You're wrong. No one will ever fathom Agustín out; he's a loner and always will be.'

'Perhaps he's just lonely,' Gemma suggested, and she thought she was probably right.

Bianca shrugged her golden shoulders. She was dressed in expensive shorts and top in a cinnamon fabric with threads of gold running through it. She made Gemma feel very shabby in the old shirt she worked in.

'That's his choice. He could have the world if he wanted it but he chooses to hide himself away here. When Felipe and I are married we'll leave. I want to settle in New York where there's life.'

She lay emphasis on her mention of marrying Felipe and Gemma steeled herself, sensing more was coming.

'Well, aren't you going to ask what Felipe thinks of that?' Her saucer-like eyes were wide and innocent but Gemma read malice there none the less.

'I'm not interested where you spend your married life,' she was able to say with conviction.

Those eyes narrowed momentarily. 'So, you're not in love with him after all?' Bianca sounded disappointed, had probably anticipated a bit of Gemma-baiting to while away some time. 'Just after his money, were you?'

'I have enough of my own,' Gemma told her baldly.

Bianca laughed shrilly, thinking that a great joke. 'A woman can never have enough of her own.'

Gemma stared at her. Could it be that Bianca was marrying Felipe for his money? Her curiosity outweighed all else.

'Are you in love with him?' Gemma asked openly.

Bianca let out another brittle laugh. 'I'm going to marry him, aren't I?'

It was all the answer Gemma needed. 'From what I gather, love is an option in this forthcoming marriage; take it or leave it,' she said.

'Love isn't important. Felipe and I will make a good marriage.'

'Of course—Agustín decrees it.'

'Agustín knows best!' Bianca burst out in a flash of temper. 'He's arranged a good marriage.'

'A profitable one too, for you.'

'It's the way things are in our circles,' Bianca snapped then suddenly she laughed. 'You're an outsider and had no chance with Felipe from the start, though I did panic when I found you shacked up with him. A phone call to Agustín to get him to summon us both to New York soon put paid to that, didn't it?'

Somehow Gemma wasn't surprised by that revelation. The whole family smacked of deviousness. So Bianca was capable of manipulating Agustín, was she? Clever girl. Gemma had got the impression from Agustín that it had been his idea to get them to New York to sign those papers. She was surprised by the revelation that Bianca didn't love Felipe, though. The looks she'd misinterpreted as looks of love were nothing more than panic at the thought of losing her rich fiancé.

'You'd better go now,' Gemma suggested. 'Agustín is due for another sitting.'

'I'm off. I've better things to do than waste time in this dreary place. You'll be going soon, won't you? Felipe will be pleased. He can't stand the sight of you any more. That's the power his father has over him.' She strolled out of the studio and Gemma stared after her, realising for the first time that Bianca was actually her cousin. A relative she could happily live without.

So Felipe couldn't stand the sight of her, Gemma reflected. Well, it was probably true, but the thought was cold comfort.

Gemma walked in the open double doors of the study. They'd been open a lot since she'd started the portrait. Agustín used the walkway every time he came for his sitting now and Gemma supposed that that was the way he had planned it: him working in the study, her mother across at the studio, close yet able to follow their own occupations. So what had kept these two people apart, two people who had loved each other? Gemma was sure Agustín had truly loved her mother... But it wasn't Agustín she had come to see; he was taking time out to tend his orchids and Felipe was working in the study.

'Agustín said to ask you for some photos of an oil rig.' Her voice was controlled and level but she'd had to work at it. She'd scarcely seen him since he'd ripped the towel from her to reveal all her failings. She would probably need some sort of counselling when she got back to England. She wasn't real, she lived in fantasy land, as Felipe had once said. She still loved him and that was unreal and a form of madness, surely?

Felipe looked up at her from the computer and frowned. 'What on earth for?'

'Background. He insists on an oil rig in the background of the portrait and, as I've never seen one in my life before, apart from on the television, I thought I'd better swot up.'

Felipe shrugged. 'I don't suppose he told you where I might find them?'

'The safe,' Gemma told him. How near normal they were.

'Here, there's a wodge of them. You'll have to sort them out.' Felipe straightened up from the safe, a monstrously old-fashioned free-standing model that looked like a safe-cracker's dream. He handed her the package and their fingers glanced off each other and the room was filled with a *frisson* of heat and awareness.

He smiled thinly. 'We can't escape from it, can we?'

Gemma looked up at him painfully. Just one tiny contact and the flame ignited and they were trapped in a ring of fire. She denied it, though.

'I don't know what you mean——'

'You do. I don't know why you persist in denying it. I thought the night we spent together——'

'Shut up!' Gemma cried, so explosively that she shocked herself. 'If you read anything into that night, forget it...' She couldn't bear to be reminded of it, their lovemaking, so perfect, so sensual, so erotic... She closed her eyes and shook her head to free herself. 'It was nothing, Felipe, it meant nothing——'

Suddenly he was in front of her, gripping her arms. Terrified, she blinked open her eyes.

'It was damn near everything!' he bit out. 'We didn't give each other our all for bloody nothing!'

'Who the hell are you kidding?' Gemma stormed back. 'Don't try and make something out of our weakness. You used me, Felipe, then you threw Bianca in my face, just as you did in London!'

'It was Bianca's idea to bring forward her trip. When you arrived here I couldn't bear the thought of her coming at all and tried to get Agustín to get rid of her but he wouldn't. She's family, after all. Agustín arranged to bring her from Caracas and that was nothing to do with me. I don't want Bianca; I never have. I meant it when I said you were my life.'

Helplessly she stared up at him. So that was who he was referring to on the phone to Agustín. She could almost believe him. Dear God, she did believe him ... but no ...

'It's all changed,' she uttered weakly, lowering her eyes. 'It's all over. I keep telling you that but you won't accept it.'

He held her for a full minute. Neither spoke but Gemma guessed his mind must be racing as wildly as hers. Finally she had got it through to him that their affair was over. Honourably? At least she still held her terrible secret and she hadn't hurt him with the truth of it. She alone would take that misery to the grave with her.

He let her go at last and sat down at his computer. 'Let me have the pictures back when you've done with them,' he said coldly, dismissively.

Gemma left him and walked slowly back to the studio, the wodge of photos clutched to her chest, a numbness creeping into her bones and her mind. She should feel elated. It was over. She was free. Free but for the guilt and shame that would be with her forever.

She poured herself some fruit juice and sat down on a couch to go through the photos. There were a lot, most extremely boring unless you were in the oil know-how. She studied them intently none the less; anything to take her mind away from Felipe.

Some of the photos were pretty old, sepia-tinted pictures of men and women who were probably family. She managed a smile. With all his money you would think Agustín de Navas could afford a decent album to mount them in. Gemma put some aside that were worth considering—and then her face paled.

Slowly she got to her feet and padded across the room to the window where there was more light. The picture was of her mother. The young, happy, beautiful Isobel Villiers. She was laughing and so obviously in love that Gemma covered her mouth with the tips of her fingers to suppress a small moan.

'What have you there?'

Gemma swung round, fumbled to get the picture behind her back.

'Let me have it, Gemma,' Agustín insisted softly.

With trembling fingers she handed it to him. He took it and stared at it painfully.

It was a long time before he spoke. 'Where did you get this?'

'It...it was in the pile of photos Felipe took from the safe.'

Agustín took one last look at the picture before ripping it in half. A cry of protest came to Gemma's shocked lips and Agustín's eyes darkened.

Gemma stared at him fearfully. 'Why...why did you do that?' Her cry of protest had been enough to rouse his suspicions without the question to follow it. Gemma tried to cover herself. 'That...that was the woman you built this studio for, wasn't it? The woman you loved?' Days ago she wouldn't have dreamed of being so open with him.

'I should have known better,' he said, almost to himself. He took up his position on the hard-backed chair and Gemma noted he still had the fragments of her mother's picture in his hand.

Gemma took up her palette, dismayed to find her fingers shaking. Agustín's tearing the picture had shocked her. He had done it with bitterness and she longed to know why. Dared she just ask? Confident in their new ease and friendship she did.

'I'd like to hear about her,' she ventured, willing the trembling of her fingers away so she could work.

Agustín smiled. 'You women, you love to gossip. Do you really want to hear the story?'

Gemma nodded—it was all she could do. Words lay inert in her throat.

'I met her in England, loved her, thought she loved me . . .'

She did and she still does, Gemma said to herself.

'I was summoned back to my country and expected her to wait for me, but she didn't. She married, had a child, a beautiful daughter.'

Gemma's fingers tightened round her brush and her heart thudded so loudly she thought he must hear it too. How did he know that her mother had married and borne a daughter?

'You went back for her?' If he had, it had been too late, just as Felipe's phone call after a week had been too late.

'Not for a long while,' Agustín went on. 'When I arrived back in Venezuela it was to find my father dying, with a company crisis on his hands. During my absence in Europe he had found a wife for me, a wife whose family could bail De Navas Oil out of trouble. Because he was so ill, I agreed, hoping that I could sort out the problems before he died and before we lost the company and then I wouldn't have to marry her.' He sighed deeply. 'Time was running out, weeks ran into months as I frantically fought for control of the company and all the time the woman I loved was waiting for my return. During one of my father's respite periods I flew back to England. Isobel had gone. I hired detectives to find her.'

'Did they?' Gemma husked, fighting back tears for her mother. She had a good idea what was coming and her heart ached for the pain of it all.

'Yes, she was found,' Agustín stated briskly. 'Married. She had wasted little time in finding a new lover and bearing his child. I was incensed, yet still I drove down to Surrey to the address I had been given. I found her, playing with her beautiful daughter in the garden of her home, looking radiant as only you English women can. I watched them from my car but made no attempt to speak with her. I knew then that it would never have worked for us. Her love hadn't been strong enough to wait for me.'

'Perhaps you should have written or phoned and told her what was happening when you first got back to Venezuela,' Gemma suggested. Her mother would have waited if she had known the hardship he had been going through, just as she, Gemma, would have waited for Felipe if only he had called her sooner from New York, but in her and Felipe's case thank God he hadn't made such a call.

'I wrote...' Gemma jerked up her head at that '...but heard nothing. At the time I thought nothing of it. Our love was strong enough...'

'She might not have got the letter,' Gemma blurted, sure that her mother never had. If she had she would have written back, she would have waited for him. She had loved him. God, was it possible that they had been deprived of love and happiness through a lost letter? That only happened in books and films, surely?

Agustín's broad shoulders heaved in a dismissive shrug. 'It made no difference. I saw the truth then. It was as I told you before...'

He paused and so did Gemma, her brush suspended in mid-air. 'What?' she murmured.

'It's best to stick to your own kind. Isobel and I were from different cultures. A South American woman would have waited till the end of time for the man she truly loved. Isobel's love wasn't deep enough. She found love again too soon.'

Isobel was pregnant, Gemma wanted to cry, carrying your child! Twenty-six years ago life was so very different...twenty-six years ago... A sudden thought nagged at the periphery of her mind. It persisted till Gemma felt slightly sick and dizzy. But not now, she couldn't work it out now...

'You married the woman your father wanted for you?' Gemma urged on softly. She had to know it all now.

'There was nothing else left for me to do. I had lost all the fight in me. I gave my father what he wanted: peace of mind to take with him to his grave.'

'But this studio. Why did you build it if you knew you were going to marry another woman?'

Agustín smiled. 'What an inquisitive mind you have. If I told you you wouldn't believe me.'

'Try me.'

'You will not laugh?'

'Is it funny?'

'You might think so. You might think the whole romantic notion a trifle incredible coming from a hardened old bastard like me.'

Gemma grinned. 'Go on, let me be the judge of whether it's funny or not.' How could anything in her

life ever be amusing again? The story he had told her
had been heartrending, a tragedy that never should
have happened. But it had, and the repercussions
Agustín would never know.

'After a week with Isobel I knew I loved her. One
week and I knew I wanted her in my life for ever.
Don't you find that amusing?'

Gemma shook her head, her eyes stinging with
tears, fuzzing the portrait before her. One week. She
swallowed hard. Funny? It was ironically heart-
breaking!

'I arranged the construction of this studio after
knowing her for only one week. It was to be a surprise
for her. She was an artist, like you, and I wanted it
to be a wedding present for her. I never told her, never
got round to proposing; we were too in love to talk
of the future.'

Gemma turned away to the sink on the pretence of
oiling her brushes. Tears burned down her cheek and
she flicked them away with the back of her hand. She
heard him move behind her and she drew herself up,
fought the sadness inside her that was tearing her
apart.

She swung to face him and he smiled down at her,
tilting her chin. 'So you did find my confessions
amusing?'

He had mistaken the mist of sadness in her eyes for
laughter. She shook her head. 'No, Agustín, not funny
but sad. I understand, you see. A week was all Felipe
and I had.'

'And you were misled into thinking it was the real
thing——'

'No!' Gemma protested, ready to argue that it had
been time enough.

'Yes, dear Gemma,' he insisted. 'Real love lasts. My love went on and I suffered for it. I love my son, we argue, we fight, it's sometimes a sign of a deep love, but I don't want him to suffer as I did. My love was betrayed by Isobel and though I'm not saying you did likewise to Felipe you must understand that European women are not the same as our own. Felipe will be happy and safer with one of his own kind.'

'You weren't happy with your own kind,' Gemma quietly retaliated.

'I made the best of it. It was better than the dishonour of having a fickle wife such as Isobel would have turned out to be.'

That hurt. Her mother had not been fickle. She had done what she thought was best at the time, married a good man to give the illegitimate child she was carrying a future. There it was again, that nagging thought that wouldn't go away...

'The session is over, I think,' Agustín said with a smile. To her surprise he bent and lightly kissed her forehead. 'I will miss you when you leave, dear Gemma. I have greatly enjoyed our sessions.'

She called out to him as he reached the door. 'Agustín.'

He turned and faced her, her father.

'If you felt that Isobel had betrayed your love, why didn't you tear down this place?'

He looked at her hard and his face was drawn, a glint of moisture on his brow the only brightness to his features. He answered at last, his voice echoing in the high, vaulted ceiling. 'I really don't know, Gemma.'

*   *   *

She had to find Maria. Maria knew all the answers in the Villa Verde household. That nagging thought in the back of her mind was swiftly developing into a hefty headache.

Though why concern herself with something that was none of her business? But she'd always been a curious creature, and she longed to know who Felipe's mother was, for sure as eggs were eggs the woman Agustín had married wasn't Felipe's mother!

She was amazed at herself for not working it out sooner, but hadn't her mind been otherwise occupied with torture and torment and bitter revenge?

She was twenty-six and Felipe thirty-two and that added up to Felipe being a bastard in the true sense of the word.

'Gemma, have you seen Mike?' Christina asked, running up to Gemma in the rose garden.

'No, I haven't. In fact I'm looking for your mother—is she around?' Gemma had ventured into the villa for the first time in days, looking for Maria but not finding her. Now she was searching the grounds and Christina appeared to be doing likewise for Mike, though Christina seemed anxious where Gemma's searching was marginally more unhurried.

Christina shrugged. 'I don't know, I look for Mike.' She frowned and muttered something in Spanish that Gemma didn't understand but the tone indicated a few expletives.

'Have you tried the tennis courts?' Gemma suggested, remembering she'd seen Mike and Bianca knocking around there earlier but that was ages ago.

'I look there.' She ran off and Gemma watched her go, puzzled by her anxiety. Seconds later she understood why.

Gemma stopped dead as she rounded the gardens by the pool and then drew back behind a screen of potted ferns. She hadn't seen that, surely? It was her eyes playing tricks in the sunlight! She hadn't seen Mike and Bianca locked in each other's arms under the shade of the cypress trees, she couldn't have!

'You're putting me in one helluva position, Bianca,' Mike growled, pulling Bianca's arms from around his neck. 'I've told you it's not on——'

Bianca's eyes darkened furiously. 'Don't tell me you prefer a servant to me——'

'Keep your voice down!' Mike hissed. 'Listen, Bianca, you're a sweet kid but it's more than my life's worth to get involved with you.'

'It'll be more than your job's worth if you don't!'

'You're just bored. You don't need me.'

'I do. You're right, Felipe is so boring——'

'You're going to marry him!'

'So! That shouldn't make any difference to us . . .'

Gemma turned away, her heart thudding furiously. Was there no one normal at the Villa Verde? Poor Mike, being blackmailed into an affair with Bianca. Did he have the strength to fight it? Resolutely she scooped her heavy hair from her face. She couldn't begin to take on anyone else's problems, she had enough of her own to last her several lifetimes. She put off her search for Maria and slowly made her way back to the studio.

Gemma stood back from the canvas. Nightfall was approaching and she had done all she could for the day. She was exhausted. She unclipped the photo of the oil rig she had been referring to from the top of the easel and slid it into the envelope with the other

photos. She must remember to return them to Felipe.
Because she was tired she started slightly as she heard
a step behind her.

'Mike!' She smiled, hesitantly. 'Have you come to
look at the portrait?'

Hadn't everyone? Even the gardeners had peeked
in. The studio Agustín had locked up for so many
years was more like a bus terminal now with people
coming and going. It saddened her to think that after
she'd gone Agustín would probably shut it up again.

'It's great,' Mike said but there was no enthusiasm
in his voice. Gemma suddenly knew why he had come.
Her shoulders sagged with weariness. She really didn't
want to be an agony aunt at this time of night.

'It's all right, Mike,' she said quietly. 'I know why
you're here. I saw you and Bianca in the gardens
today.'

Mike gave her a crooked smile and sank down on
to a couch. 'I could do with a coffee,' he told her,
raking his fingers through his spiky blond hair.

'I'll put the water on,' Gemma murmured kindly.

It all came out, the whole story. Mike being Mike,
outgoing and sociable, had given Bianca the wrong
impression. She had taken his zest for life as a personal zest for her and reacted by throwing herself at
him wholeheartedly.

'I don't want her, Gemma. It's Christina I'm crazy
about. How can I get out of it and keep my job? She'll
do for me, the spoilt little bitch.'

'You'll just have to beat her to Agustín, that's all.
Go to him and tell him she's sexually harassing you
at work and it isn't on.'

They both laughed and then Mike grew serious.
'And if he doesn't believe me I'm out.'

'And if you don't give Bianca what she wants, you're out! Take your pick—go with your head held high or your tail between your legs. You know what you have to do and really you didn't need me to confirm it.'

'I needed to share it, though. There was no one else I could talk to. You're detached from the whole family and not emotionally involved with them and that's why I came to you.'

That must be the understatement of the century, Gemma thought dismally. Loneliness engulfed her.

Mike stood up and on impulse leaned forward, gripped her shoulders and gave her a big kiss on the cheek. 'Thanks for being there,' he murmured. 'And I think the picture's swell.'

Gemma smiled wanly as he strode out of the open door. That was her good deed done for the day, though she wondered if she'd done the right thing in suggesting he go to Agustín with the problem. It would cause a row and hadn't there been enough of that lately?

She turned to the sink to rinse out their coffee-cups, dismissing the problem from her mind. It wasn't hers; why should she lose sleep over it? She heard a step behind her. Who now? She could make a fortune standing on the door taking entrance money.

'Mike now, eh? Very bloody cosy!'

Gemma didn't even turn to look at him but she tensed inside. So he'd seen Mike leaving, for all she knew he'd seen that kiss too. More harassment? She couldn't take any more. 'Yes, Mike,' she sighed wearily. 'Quite insatiable, aren't I? I wonder where I get the energy from sometimes.'

'Is that supposed to be funny?' Felipe swung her round to face him, his eyes silvered with rage.

'I thought it was pretty hilarious!'

'Have you no pride——?'

'No,' she spat back at him. 'You wear my pride as a loincloth...'

'Dear God, but you're evil!'

'Dear God, but you're a damned saint!' she hit back sarcastically.

'I don't take the servants' lovers!'

'Well, someone does, but it isn't me! I suggest you search closer to home!' Gemma immediately regretted that. Much as she detested Bianca, she had no intention of snitching on her.

'What do you know?' Felipe growled.

'Nothing!' Gemma told him, tight-lipped, sweeping her hair from her face, at the same time hurling his hands from her arms.

'Was that why he was here? Confiding in you that he had a new lover?'

'He loves Christina...'

'He's seeing someone else. This is a close community and there's gossip. If you know something you'd better spit it out.'

She supposed that was something. He actually believed that she wasn't Mike's new lover. How she'd love to tell him it was his precious, precocious fiancée seeing Mike behind Christina's back, but she couldn't, of course—that would bring her down to their mudslinging level!

'To hell with you, Felipe. You can think what you please. You'll get nothing from me!'

'It's Bianca, isn't it?' he let out on a long breath. 'My, God, I'll kill the bastard!'

He went to turn away and Gemma lunged at him and grasped his bare arm. She let it go as quickly as she'd grasped it.

'Leave it, Felipe.' She licked her dry lips, wondering why she was bothering, but she liked Mike and the only fault he had was a weakness for allowing Bianca to manipulate him this far already. 'It's not Mike's fault. He really cares for Christina...' Her voice frayed. That was admission enough that it was Bianca. So what did she care? No one ever took her feelings into account when they were dishing out the dirt.

'Are you saying that Bianca is making a play for Mike?' His voice was low and loaded with disbelief.

'I said nothing of the sort,' she retorted. Whatever she said she couldn't win. She was the wicked witch of the north and that was that! 'I want no part of all this. I'm tired. Leave me alone.'

Felipe snorted with rage. 'I suppose it's all I should expect from you. Plant a few seeds of dissent and walk away to let them flourish in someone else's mind.'

Gemma had to laugh. 'OK, I take full responsibility. It's all *my* fault—now will you get out of here and let me get some rest?'

'Is Bianca making a play for Mike?' he repeated, grasping her arm to add weight to the question, as if his tone wasn't weighty enough.

Gemma's eyes hardened and defied him. 'If she is, that would really hit you below the belt, wouldn't it?'

His eyes pierced hers with such intensity that she blinked painfully.

'The only pain I suffer in that region is when I'm within striking distance of you, sweet one, and I'm not speaking metaphorically,' he gibed.

Gemma's breath caught in her throat. When would this end, this constant pressure on her senses? She tried to wrest her arm from his, resorted to using her free hand to prise his fingers from her.

'You're stopping my blood flow...I've a portrait to finish tomorrow...'

'That soon.' His grip eased but only long enough to manoeuvre her into a more accessible position. Suddenly she was in his arms.

'Then there is still much to be done,' he breathed sensuously at her throat.

God, he hadn't given up! She felt the fiery heat all over her body, from her head to her toes. It tore fearfully through her, scorching every nerve-ending in its path, as his hands lowered and gripped her hips to draw her into him. As their bodies made terrifying, electrifying contact she opened her mouth to scream but nothing happened and then the pressure was off and she felt as if she had been sucked out from an aircraft flying at thirty thousand feet and was hurling through space.

She opened her eyes, dizzily, not sure if she was alive or dead. She saw Felipe's retreating figure and Maria, God bless her, standing in the doorway with her supper tray.

Life flooded back into Gemma's veins. Trembling, she turned to the sink as Maria came across the studio floor.

Maria was blushing as she came to stand beside her. 'I sorry, Gemma. I should bang on the door. I didn't mean to...'

Gemma forced a laugh. 'It doesn't matter, Maria.' You saved my life, Gemma added inwardly. But what must she be thinking? Gemma thought wearily. She

knew the family, knew that Bianca was promised to
Felipe, knew that there was something going on be-
tween her and Felipe ... Gemma exhaled a deep sigh.
She wanted to go home, away from all this horror.

'Is nearly finished,' Maria commented as she peered
at the portrait of Agustín, and Gemma had to admire
her discretion. Maybe that was why she had survived
so many years with this twisted family.

'Is funny.'

Gemma frowned. 'What do you mean, funny?'

'Is like you.'

Gemma paled, sank down on to the couch before
the weakness in her legs sagged her to the floor. She
hadn't imagined for a minute ... She stared at the
canvas. No, it wasn't possible ... but it was. Suddenly
she saw it, the likeness. Very subtle, something in the
eyes, the line of the cheekbones ...

'I think there is always something of the artist in
his or her own work,' Gemma mouthed, her lips
working on automatic pilot. She uncovered the tray
Maria had brought her, stared at the food unseeingly.
Maria had seen it—had anyone else? No, it was impossible. She hadn't seen it herself till it was pointed
out to her ...

'Maria?'

'Si.' Maria turned from the canvas. Her eyes looked
troubled and Gemma aborted the question that was
on the tip of her tongue. Instead she said, 'Don't
worry about Mike and Christina. They love each other
very much and everything is going to be all right.'

Maria nodded and smiled. 'Si, I know, but ... but
you and Felipe ...' She shook her head as if it was all
hopeless. 'I see, Gemma, but I no understand. I see
the love ...'

'Don't, Maria,' Gemma pleaded. How could she have seen love? They had fought non-stop from the minute she had arrived at the Hammer House of Horror.

She resurrected the question she had been about to ask. 'Maria, you've known the family a long time. Who was Felipe's mother?' After all that Felipe had dished out to her she was still curious—or did she just want to divert attention away from the treacherous thoughts of her and Felipe that kept flashing across her mind?

Maria shrugged and put the pan on for Gemma's coffee. 'I don't know, no one knows. All we know is that she was a bad woman.'

'She left her son to be raised by his father?' Gemma supposed that was bad in this proud country.

'No, the father he bad too...'

Agustín, bad? Surely not—he'd given him the best of everything.

'Felipe's parents sell the drugs on the streets of Bogota. Felipe, a child, he take the drugs. He sick and thin and poor and he die if Señor de Navas...'

Gemma eyes widened till they hurt. Something inside her swelled with hope. 'Maria,' she husked pitifully, 'are you telling me Felipe is *not* Agustín's son?'

Maria shook her head and Gemma let go of the straw she had clutched at so desperately.

'They father and son, is true. Señor de Navas make the... the *adopcíon*...'

'Adopted! Felipe is adopted!' Gemma cried, grabbing back the straw and clasping it to her heart. She felt sick and dizzy and happy and... 'But I don't understand...' Where had her thinking been when all

this had cropped up? Felipe wasn't a de Navas, he
was a Santos. 'But Maria, he is a Santos.'

'*Si*, we have many names. Santos is Felipe's family
but he have de Navas too. Felipe's mother and father
they die soon after Señor de Navas take Felipe from
the street. He make him his own son, the *señora* have
no children, it not possible so Felipe the child he
want...'

Gemma felt floaty and weak inside. Felipe wasn't
her half-brother, was no blood relative whatsoever.
They had committed no sin. She had nothing to feel
guilty or shameful or disgusted about. She was happy,
but she wasn't. Her mind raced frantically. And then
as swiftly as her euphoria had risen it deflated like a
burst balloon. This dear, sweet, wonderful news was
too late. The love she had once shared with Felipe
had gone. Torment and bitterness and fear had
poisoned it and all that remained was a sourness that
couldn't be sweetened. It was too far gone to be
salvaged.

CHAPTER NINE

FELIPE'S mouth was tender and loving, his tongue warm and sensual.

'This is how it should be,' Gemma murmured, basking in his caresses, moving languidly against him as his hands smoothed over her hips urging her to his body. 'No more fighting, Felipe,' she breathed plaintively.

'No more torment, *querida*. I love you, you are my life.'

She guided him into her sweet warmth and he moved gently, pressing into her and covering her face and neck with erotic kisses. She clung to him, holding him to her body and her heart, never to let him go. He was hers and always would be. His penetration deepened and quickened and suddenly she was in pain. A fierce, cruel, wicked pain.

'You're hurting me!'

He laughed, thrust harder.

'No...no, you mustn't! Felipe...you can't...'

She felt him swell inside her and screamed in terror.

'No...no...you're my brother...'

Her screams woke her. Perspiration matted the sheet to her trembling body. Her breath came in long desperate gasps of fear. She was so hot and there was no air and that noise... Oh, God, a nightmare...so real...

She held her head in her hands till the sobs receded. He wasn't her half-brother; she had done no wrong. She had nothing to fear...and yet she had everything to fear. Nightmares had their roots in reality. She hadn't made love with her half-brother but the shame and guilt were still there because she wasn't at all sure that she could have resisted him even if he had been. The thought was like a sickness inside her. Felipe's torment. It would never go away.

Achingly she untangled her legs from the sheet. That noise again, so persistent, a rushing sound. It was light, she realised, sweeping her tousled hair from her damp face. Her head started to clear. It was raining. Water was rushing down the sloping roof.

Gemma went to the window and watched white water lash the windowpane. It was hotter than ever and yet she shivered, not able to shake off the terror of her nightmare. Yesterday she had fought him off thinking their love was forbidden—now she was free to love him but it was hopelessly too late. She'd put an ocean between them all right, an ocean of bitterness. And Bianca...Felipe had been incensed at the thought of Mike pursuing his cousin. Why? Because he cared for her, that was why. But whom did he desire? She knew that. Herself, but sex wasn't what marriages were about. They were about loving and caring and those were two emotions Felipe hadn't house room for in his heart.

Gemma showered and dressed in skimpy shorts and the flimsiest cotton top she had. She tied her thick hair back from her shoulders with a ribbon. The humidity was stifling.

'How long will this last?' she asked Maria when she brought her breakfast tray, using the covered walkway from the study.

'Days,' Maria told her. 'Is good for the land but no good for the people. It bring trouble. The torment of the head. Already it start.'

Gemma laughed, taking the tray from her hands. 'What do you mean?'

Maria waved her work worn hands in the air. 'Trouble, always the trouble when the rains come. Señor de Navas, Felipe, Bianca, they all trouble this morning. I go and keep out of the way.'

When she'd gone Gemma took the tray to the couch by the easel and sat down to eat but had no appetite. She drank the coffee, though, realising what Maria meant by the torment of the head. Hers was beginning to thump in time to the incessant rain outside.

She stared at the nearly completed portrait as she sipped her coffee and tried to appraise it from a stranger's point of view. It was good and she wasn't being vain. It was her best work and she knew it. Tears smarted her eyes. Her mother would never see it, would never see Agustín as he was now. Distinguished, arrogant, proud...another session and she would have no reason to see him again either.

What a waste, Gemma mused. Their love lost, just like her and Felipe's.

'*Puta! Lagarta!*'

Gemma swung round. Bianca. She hadn't heard her approach and fear stiffened her spine at the girl's rage.

'You spiteful bitch! You went to my uncle and told him everything!' Her eyes blazed with such inky hatred that Gemma shot to her feet.

She was confused at first and then it dawned on her what this was about. So Mike had told Agustín...or maybe... No, not Felipe. His pride wouldn't allow him to acknowledge to his father that his bride-to-be was messing with someone else.

'I don't know what you're talking about...' She did, of course, but a dumbstruck approach was safer, Bianca looked ready to tear her hair out.

'Of course you do, that's why you did it! To make things bad for me and Felipe. You can't accept that he doesn't want you, can you? You were so damned jealous you just had to spoil it for me. Everyone you wanted for yourself, even my uncle.'

'Bianca, stop. You don't know what you're saying——'

'I know exactly what I'm saying. Someone told my uncle about me and Mike and it had to be you and don't deny you didn't know because Mike said you had seen us in the gardens. He tried to finish with me saying it was unsafe because you had seen us but you had to put the knife in, didn't you?'

Suddenly Gemma was exhausted despite the early hour, exhausted by this continual tirade on her nerves.

'I had nothing to do with any of this,' she protested.

Bianca swung to the portrait and accused it with her finger. 'All the time you were doing *that* you were trying for Agustín. You couldn't have Felipe so you tried seducing his father——'

'No!' Gemma cried. She couldn't take this. Now Bianca believed she wanted Agustín.

'Oh, yes! You're nothing but an English whore——'

Something inside Gemma snapped. She turned to get away, felt a rush of hot air close to her and strong arms gripping her.

'Bianca!' The name came like a roar in the jungle and Bianca twisted round in fright, catching her leg against the easel.

Gemma spun out of Felipe's grip to clutch at the canvas before it crashed to the ground. It all went down, the easel, the canvas, crashing to the pine floor. Gemma stared down at in horror and then with a sob she dropped to her knees next to the canvas.

'Get out!' Felipe roared. 'Pack your bags and be ready to leave immediately!'

Gemma jerked her head up, her heart in traction. He believed Bianca, believed that she wanted Agustín and now he was ordering her out. But he wasn't looking at her. His fearful dark eyes were on Bianca.

'I'm not going, Felipe,' Bianca bleated. 'Agustín said we were going to work this out——'

'I'm giving the orders, not Agustín. Do as I say and prepare to leave.' He turned to Gemma and lifted her from her knees. She stood against him, too shocked to move.

'You're making a mistake, Felipe,' Bianca cried in desperation. 'She's a sneak, telling lies about me to Agustín...she's crazy about *him*, not you...' She stopped as Felipe's face darkened murderously and then with a deep sob she turned and ran out of the studio.

The rain, lashing the windows and the roof, drowned out all sound but Felipe's ragged breath against her.

Slowly Gemma moved out of the circle of his arms, pushing at his hands with trembling fingers. She only allowed her mind to be concerned about the portrait, all else was a fog of confusion. She stooped to pick it up...

Felipe pulled her back from it, his breath now harsh on her face. 'She's right, it's him you care more for than me.'

Her eyes shot flames of fire at him. For one hopeless moment she had thought he was on her side. 'I've worked hard on this portrait. If it's damaged——'

'You'll have to paint it again,' he sneered. 'And that should please you, give you more time with your lover.'

She stared up at him, numb with shock that he could still believe such a thing.

'Do you love him?' The question was torn out of his throat and his hands fastened so tightly round her arms that it drew her shoulders up with pain.

Her eyes were dark and wide with anguish and she knew she couldn't take any more. She knew that he'd won and he'd destroyed her. All his threats and promises to leave her a broken woman had happened. But she couldn't take his last torment.

'Yes, I love him,' she cried desperately, and his grip nearly snapped her arms. 'Yes, I love him, because ... because he's my father!'

Her shoulders sagged as he let her go, brutally, as if she were aflame and he would get scorched if he held on to her a second longer. She held his eyes, his cold, shocked, implacable eyes. She was crying but could do nothing to stop it.

'What are you saying?' Felipe grated in disbelief.

Gemma shook her head from side to side. She couldn't speak. She'd said enough and it was far too much. She turned and ran from the studio, not stopping even when he roared her name.

She was soaked through to the skin as soon as she dashed outside but she didn't care. All that mattered was escape, to get as far away from him as she could. She ran, not knowing where. Lightning speared the air around her and on a scream of terror she sprinted to the nearest shelter.

Gemma threw herself through an open doorway and landed in a bed of warm yellow straw. Stunned, she lay there gasping for breath, and then more terror spurred through her.

'Stay where you are!'

Gemma heard and obeyed and lay coiled and still in the straw.

Felipe soothed the spooked stallion with soft words of comfort, his hands caressing the animal's muzzle. The black horse whinnied nervously and shifted his hoofs restlessly, dangerously close to Gemma's paralysed form. Slowly Felipe stroked the stallion to calmness while Gemma cringed in fear.

'Get in the next stall, slowly and without sudden movement,' Felipe said calmly, and it was seconds before she realised he was talking to her.

Gemma looked up and saw that she was lying by a closed stable door that led to the next stall. She inched her way to it on her knees, keeping her fearful eyes on the horse, groping to find the door with trembling hands. Slowly she stood up, her back to the worn wood, her fingers fumbling for the catch. She found it at last, it gave easily, and, holding her breath, she backed through the door, slowly, carefully, easing it shut behind her.

She collapsed on to fresh straw and let the tension and fear seep out from her body. Minutes later she felt comforting arms around her, lifting her to sit up in her bed of straw. She blinked open her eyes and pressed her face hard against Felipe's wet shirt.

'It's all right. You're safe. You scared him more than he scared you.'

'You ... you wouldn't like to put money on that, would you?' she husked. What a time to joke. She must be mad! She *was* mad, clinging to him like this. She tried to move away but he wouldn't allow it.

'No more running, Gemma.' He smoothed her wet hair from her face, wiped the raindrops from her chin with the back of his fingers. 'You can't drop a

statement like that and make a dash for it. There's
nowhere to run to.'

She shook her head miserably. 'I...I shouldn't have
said...I didn't mean...'

He stilled her shuddering shoulders with his hands.
'Look at me, Gemma. Tell me this is a dream.'

'A nightmare!' she sobbed, lowering her head, not
able to look at him.

He made her, forced up her chin. 'Why did you say
what you did?'

She looked at him then, she had no choice. He
didn't believe her and why should he? It was all too
fantastic for belief.

'You said you loved Agustín because he was your
father. Gemma, tell me, tell me what all this is about.'

'Why?' she blurted. 'So you can laugh at me,
torment me, hurt me even more than you already
have!' She tried to struggle up from the straw but he
hauled her down beside him, held her wrist so she
couldn't move.

'I don't want to hurt you, Gemma——'

'You have! You do! All the time! You never let up
on me——'

'Because I'm crazy about you!' he growled. 'Can't
you see the damned torment you put *me* through? I
love you so much I'm out of my mind with it...' He
stopped, let her go, sat raking his fingers through his
dripping wet hair. 'I love you so much I could kill
you for it——'

'You should have done,' she cried, 'months ago and
then I wouldn't have suffered so! You brought me
here to torment me, Felipe, and you did, more than
you could ever have imagined. Agustín *is* my father.
I'm the love child of him and Isobel Villiers, the
woman your father built the studio for...and...and

if that isn't bad enough to live with, I found you were his son . . . I loved my brother . . . had *made* love with my brother . . .'

She thought he *would* kill her then. He turned on her with rage and fire in his eyes, spurred by the shock of her stuttered outpourings. She tried to scramble to her feet but he grabbed at her ankle, felling her with one twist of his powerful hand. She lay there, in the warm straw, stunned, and he straddled her, holding her wrists above her head.

'What madness is this?' he raged at the top of his voice.

Gemma squirmed helplessly under him. 'It's true!' she panted. 'I didn't know till I got this commission but he *is* my father——'

'And you thought I was your brother . . . and you let me make love to you!'

'I didn't know you were adopted then . . . I didn't know till . . .'

'Till when?' Felipe raged and Gemma knew what was going through his demented mind.

'You bastard!' she raged.

'Tell me! Our night of love—did it come before or after you knew I wasn't your real brother?'

Gemma brought her knee up into his back and for a brief second his hold on her wavered. She brought her hands up and heaved at his chest. It was like trying to move a small mountain. She couldn't fight him with her strength but there was plenty of power in her words.

'Neither, you . . . you perverted rat, and don't you mean our night of torment, not love?'

'I know what it was but do you, sweet one? Have you any idea what you put me through——?'

'Huh, nothing to what you've put me through. No, I didn't love you that night knowing I was committing ... committing incest, I didn't even know you were Agustín's son, real or otherwise, and I don't care if you believe me or not because I hate you!'

'*Dios mío!*' he breathed so deeply that Gemma thought it was his last breath. Then he lifted her up into his arms and buried his face in her wet hair. 'I've done this to you,' he grated fiercely. 'Dear God, Gemma, what can I do to put all this right?'

She clasped him to her, tears mingling with the raindrops dripping from her hair to her face, their soaking bodies moulded together in the cloying heat of the stables. 'Felipe,' she moaned, and it was a cry of sheer desperation.

He held her for a long time, their hearts thudding against each other, the rain echoing the beat in the sudden stillness of the storm as its power weakened.

Gemma was the first to move. Hesitantly because she was still afraid, not of him, but of herself. She had suffered so much and she still hurt inside. Her guilt and shame had left its mark and she would never be free of this anguish.

'I have to tell you everything, Felipe,' she whispered huskily. 'About Agustín and my mother...'

'And us, Gemma,' he urged. 'We must talk about ourselves, we must stop this torment with each other...'

She gave a small smile through her tears. 'I didn't know I was tormenting you too.'

'More than you'll ever know. London was complete and then nothing after that, like a living death. Not a moment passed without me poisoning myself with believing you didn't care for me.'

'I always loved you, Felipe, and I hurt so badly
when you left. I now know why you had to go to New
York; Agustín said you had papers to sign...'

'Yes, he summoned us both and wanted us there
immediately. I didn't get a chance to call you before
we left and then when we arrived it was far more de-
tailed than I expected. It was one of those family con-
ferences that always seemed to get put off for more
pressing matters but suddenly Agustín wanted it
settled there and then. He has a vast empire and
Bianca and I are his only family...' His voice trailed
at what he had just said.

Gemma was family too now, but she said nothing
and she said nothing about Bianca's confession that
she had manipulated Agustín into that summons to
New York. There had been enough trouble and harsh
words already and it was best left alone.

'I didn't know that at the time, Felipe. I just thought
you cared for Bianca and not me. Then...then you
arranged the commission and I found out about my
father...'

His lips on hers caressed away her distressed words
and slowly, slowly she felt the tension ease a little.
The freedom to love, it whispered in her heart, and
she knew it to be true, but the suffering couldn't be
swept out of her tortured mind just like that. She
moved her mouth from his and pressed it to his cheek.

'Please, Felipe, please let me talk.'

He cradled her in his arms against the straw, kissing
the top of her head as she started, haltingly, striving
to sound lucid but sometimes failing so miserably that
nothing came from her lips at all. She knew when her
story troubled him; the kisses stopped and she felt the
tension stiffen him. Tears punctuated her narrative

and that was when he smoothed his hands over her cheeks to console her.

'And you've not spoken of all this to Agustín?' he said at last.

'How could I? I couldn't just spring a daughter on him like that; besides after all he told me he thinks my mother betrayed him...'

'As you betrayed me,' Felipe murmured, and she turned to him with dismay in her wide brown eyes.

'As you *thought* I'd betrayed you, Felipe. Can't you see the irony of it all? History repeating itself and all that.'

He tightened his arms around her. 'But history isn't going to be allowed to repeat itself, because I'll never let you go——'

'Agustín will never allow it——'

Felipe let out a rumble of laughter. 'He can't stop us, *querida*. I love you and I intend to marry you and put us both out of our misery for evermore.'

'But Bianca——'

'Bianca was nothing in my life, Gemma. How could you have ever believed she was?'

'You said she was a bigger part of your life than I was.'

'Only in time. Being my cousin she's been around longer, that's all. I never had any intentions of marrying her, Agustín or not.'

'But you were furious when you thought Mike was trying to seduce her.'

'Only because I thought he was betraying Christina.'

'But...but...you used her to torment me——'

He didn't let her finish, but eased up on one elbow to gaze down at her. 'Love can be so damned destructive, my darling. I was so obsessed with you I hated you—it sounds crazy but it's true. I baited you with Bianca because I wanted you to suffer as I had.'

'You could only wish for that if you thought I really cared for you in the first place. You must have known how deeply I loved you.'

'I knew that London hadn't been a lie but I thought something had happened to change your feelings. I wanted to resurrect the passion we had known and then to destroy it, for us both. But after that night we made love I hoped, I prayed... I thought you loved me and wanted me. I knew my own love had never died, and then Agustín arrived with Bianca.'

'I thought you'd done it to add more torment and after that row at dinner I found out you were Agustín's son. Maria told me but she didn't say you were his adopted son and——'

He brushed his lips across hers. 'And you thought you'd made love to your own half-brother...'

Gemma turned her head from his, biting her lip to stop it trembling.

'Gemma,' Felipe breathed, a frown of consternation darkening his features, 'it's over. You have nothing to feel ashamed about.'

Her eyes widened and glazed with more tears. 'I have everything to feel ashamed about, Felipe,' she gasped raggedly. 'You see...even...even when I thought we were blood relatives...I...still loved you...still wanted you...'

Felipe was still for a moment. 'And if I had pushed you, really pushed you, you were afraid that you would have allowed it to happen?'

'Of course!' she blurted on a sob. 'I didn't know if I could hold back from you...'

'But you did, silly,' Felipe insisted, gripping her shoulders. 'Don't you see that you did? In the shower,

Gemma, I could have taken you then and after when I stripped the towel from you to taunt you, it would have been so easy to take you——'

'But you didn't!' Gemma insisted. 'Because you hated me by then!'

'No, I didn't hate you. I loved you more than ever and the reason I didn't make love to you was because you were stopping me. I could see it in your eyes, the fear. It was something new to me and I thought I had done that to you with my crazed torment and revenge. So you see, Gemma, you did hold me off...'

'I didn't think I had.' Could she believe him? If she was to survive she must try.

'Don't torture yourself over something that would never have happened, Gemma. That thinking is so destructive.'

She managed a watery smile and shook her head. 'That's good advice coming from you.'

He smiled back at her and held her eyes and the anxiety slid from her heart. He took her in his arms and lay her back on the straw and when his lips came to hers it dispelled the last shred of doubt.

There was no room in her heart for anything but Felipe as his kiss deepened and led her away from pain and torment. They were free to love each other without punishment or shame to mar the sweet pleasure.

There was no rush, no hurry, no fevered urgency in the prelude to their lovemaking. The power and the frantic need would come later when their control would run wild and they would go with it wherever it led them. For now there was the need to love and reassure, to explore and rediscover with hearts that were free.

Felipe slowly peeled her wet clothes from her,
laughed softly as she winced at the scratchy straw
under her naked body. He reached up and pulled a
horse blanket under her and she helped him take off
his wet shirt, his rain-soaked cotton jeans, her fingers
jerky and awkward in her haste. He knelt by her side,
naked and powerful, sleek and dark and glistening
with moisture. He was magnificent and Gemma
reached up to score her fingers down his chest, to feel
the contraction of his muscles at the thrill of her touch.
In turn he adored every inch of her body with his eyes
and his mouth and his hands and Gemma matched
every pleasure he gave her, their need to love and show
their love powering them to new heights of daring.

The control was slipping and they went with it, each
caress and stroke becoming more feverish, more
urgent. Gemma ached for him inside her, pleaded
softly for it.

Their eyes locked as he moved between her legs,
lifting her hips to take the force of his first shattering
thrust. He loved the moment of possession, that exquisite plunge into a world of liquid sensuality, a
throbbing, pressing heat that pulsed the nerves till they
clamoured furiously for that inexplicable moment of
power that was so mysterious and unique.

Gemma watched his face, revelling in the look of
triumph in his eyes, the baring of his teeth as if in
pain as he fully penetrated her at last. That look excited her deeply, raged a fire within her till it con-
sumed all reasoning. He was inside her, where he
belonged, loving her, muscular energy reassuring her
that their love was whole and beautiful and should
never have been doubted. She moved with him,
equalling his strength, urging him to the edge of
unreality.

She cried out when she could hold on no longer, when the need to let go was so furious that she thought she would die from holding back.

'I can't hold back...' she cried, arching herself against him.

'Don't try, *querida*, don't stop our love... now, my love, now!'

Together they rose and crashed through the barriers of ecstasy. Life force, golden and molten, pumped miraculously, matching their cries of release and triumph and love. They were free, soaring like eagles in a cloudless blue sky of perfection, free to be together forever and beyond.

'Felipe has told me everything.'

Gemma nervously smoothed down her painting shirt and gazed at her father as he took up his position in the hard-backed chair for the last time. The canvas hadn't suffered for its unceremonious dumping on the pine floor, but Gemma's nerves had suffered as she had waited for her father.

'I couldn't have told you,' she admitted, taking up her palette and brushes and wondering if she would ever get this portrait finished without a complete nervous breakdown. Bianca was packed and ready to go. Mike was flying her to Caracas with Maria and Christina as chaperons in case Bianca got naughty on the flight, and, oddly, Agustín was going too, en route to somewhere else, where Gemma didn't know and hadn't given much thought to. She had more important things on her mind: Felipe and what he had told his father.

'It was right that Felipe told me,' Agustín said quietly. 'I think I might have had a heart attack if you had told me yourself.'

'You might not have believed me.'

'I should have known. The hair, your strength of character, your talent, so very much like your mother. Now tell me, Gemma, tell me about your mother.'

Happily she complied. All her tension and anguish seeping from her soul as she talked and added the final strokes to the best portrait she had ever painted.

'She still loves you, you know,' she murmured at last, and suspected that that was what he had wanted to hear from the very start of her story.

Slowly he got up and came to stand next to her to look at the finished portrait, his hand resting on her shoulder. Gemma smiled and covered his hand with her own.

'I must have been blind,' he murmured as he studied the picture. 'It's all there, isn't it? The eyes, the mouth.'

'I didn't see it myself till Maria pointed it out,' Gemma laughed. 'Agustín,' she suddenly said. 'Felipe and I——'

He turned her to face him, held her hands at her side. 'It's all right. Am I such an ogre that you think I would deprive my own daughter of her happiness? You have my blessing . . .'

'But . . . you wanted one of your own kind for Felipe . . .'

'And that is precisely what he has. You're South American, dear Gemma, one of our own.'

Gemma laughed and colour rose to her face in a flush of happiness. 'Yes, of course, I keep forgetting,' she murmured.

'Now I must leave,' Agustín said, glancing at his watch. 'I have a connection to make in Caracas.'

'Business?'

He kissed her forehead. 'Unfinished business.'

'Am I permitted to ask where?' She grinned, a sparkle to her saucer-wide eyes.

He smiled secretively. 'A little village in Surrey where long ago I saw a mother and baby daughter playing in the garden on a warm summer afternoon.'

'Give her my love.' Gemma smiled happily and he nodded.

'You and Felipe will have the place to yourself for a while. Make the most of it, dear daughter, for when we return you women will have to knuckle down to being dutiful, obedient Latin American wives.'

'Don't count on it!' Gemma laughed as he walked across the studio to the door.

'Tame her,' she heard him order Felipe as they crossed in the doorway.

'What was that all about?' Felipe asked as he swept her into his arms.

'Oh, just good old-fashioned chauvinism waving its red flag. Just wait till my mother gets hold of him; he won't know what's hit him.'

'If it's a tenth of what you've hit me with I pity him,' Felipe laughed. 'It's finished, then.' He stepped back with her still in his arms to admire the portrait. 'It's good, Gemma—superb, in fact.'

'Will it be my last?' She didn't want it to be; she wanted to carry on her career.

He grinned down at her, knowing what was going through her mind. 'That's a very leading question and one we have never discussed before.'

'Perhaps we should discuss it now. There's so much we don't know about each other, Felipe, so much we haven't covered in our relationship. You know the trouble we get into when we put other things first,' she laughed.

'"Other things" being this, I suppose.' His lips rested on hers, tenderly, lovingly. His hands moved under her shirt to cup her breasts. His hands were still on her heated flesh when he drew his mouth from hers. 'Maybe in fifty years' time when we can tear ourselves out of each other's arms we'll sit down and get to know each other properly.'

'We might find we are totally incompatible,' she teased.

'By then it will be too late; we'll be in our dotage and no one else will want us.'

Gemma slid her arms around Felipe's neck. 'Then we'll truly be lumbered with each other.' She kissed his chin then gazed up at him. 'Is it going to be all right?' she murmured worriedly. 'Us, I mean?'

'What are you afraid of, Gemma? I love you, always have, since the moment I saw you across that crowded gallery floor...'

'Me too. Love at first sight and nothing but torment since. It wasn't the right way to do it, Felipe.'

'The pain and the bitterness is over, my darling. We've been lucky, hauled our love back from the brink of destruction. Agustín and your mother lost a lifetime of happiness and I'm not going to let that happen to us.'

He swept her into his arms and carried her to the day-bed, lay down beside her and gathered her into his arms. 'I'll never hurt you again, Gemma. I brought you here to punish you because the pain of my love was tying me in knots. I tormented us both with my cruelty. It will never happen again, I promise you.'

'Oh,' she breathed.

He backed off from her and looked down in puzzlement. 'You sound disappointed.'

She linked her hands around his neck, coiled her fingers in his silky curls. 'Well, there are a few torments that can be addictive.'

He grinned and slid a hand under her shirt. 'And a few we haven't found yet. But we have a lifetime to discover them, together, and we'll make a start now.'

He lowered his mouth to hers and Gemma was ready for him with her own lips parted in rapture. Revenge, torture, pain and bitterness. He had shown her it all, but now the hurt was over.

She shifted restlessly under him as his hands slid tantalisingly down her body, touching, caressing, teasing them both towards the brink of a world that was their very own. Felipe's mystical world where sensuality and hedonism were transformed into a delicious love torment that would carry them through the rest of their days.

This was the sweetest torment of all.

Next Month's Romances

Each month you can choose from a wide variety of romance with Mills & Boon. Below are the new titles to look out for next month, why not ask either Mills & Boon Reader Service or your Newsagent to reserve you a copy of the titles you want to buy – just tick the titles you would like and either post to Reader Service or take it to any Newsagent and ask them to order your books.

Please save me the following titles:		Please tick	√
BACHELOR AT HEART	Roberta Leigh		
TIDEWATER SEDUCTION	Anne Mather		
SECRET ADMIRER	Susan Napier		
THE QUIET PROFESSOR	Betty Neels		
ONE-NIGHT STAND	Sandra Field		
THE BRUGES ENGAGEMENT	Madeleine Ker		
AND THEN CAME MORNING	Daphne Clair		
AFTER ALL THIS TIME	Vanessa Grant		
CONFRONTATION	Sarah Holland		
DANGEROUS INHERITANCE	Stephanie Howard		
A MAN FOR CHRISTMAS	Annabel Murray		
DESTINED TO LOVE	Jennifer Taylor		
AN IMAGE OF YOU	Liz Fielding		
TIDES OF PASSION	Sally Heywood		
DEVIL'S DREAM	Nicola West		
HERE COMES TROUBLE	Debbie Macomber		

If you would like to order these books in addition to your regular subscription from Mills & Boon Reader Service please send £1.70 per title to: Mills & Boon Reader Service, P.O. Box 236, Croydon, Surrey, CR9 3RU, quote your Subscriber No:.....................................
(If applicable) and complete the name and address details below. Alternatively, these books are available from many local Newsagents including W.H.Smith, J.Menzies, Martins and other paperback stockists from 4th December 1992.

Name:...
Address:...
....Post Code:..........................
To Retailer: If you would like to stock M&B books please contact your regular book/magazine wholesaler for details.

You may be mailed with offers from other reputable companies as a result of this application.
If you would rather not take advantage of these opportunities please tick box ☐